Demon SLAY

KIMETSU NO YAIB

TANJIRO KAMADO

ZENITSU AGATSUMA

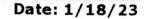
SLAYER!

KIMETSU NO YAIBA

THE FLOWER OF HAPPINESS

Novel by
AYA YAJIMA

Art and Original Concept by
KOYOHARU GOTOUGE

VIZ MEDIA   SHONEN JUMP

DEMON SLAYER: KIMETSU NO YAIBA— THE FLOWER OF HAPPINESS

Novel by
AYA YAJIMA
Original Concept and Art by
KOYOHARU GOTOUGE

TRANSLATION Jocelyne Allen
DESIGN Jimmy Presler
EDITOR Jennifer Sherman

KIMETSU NO YAIBA SHIAWASE NO HANA © 2019 by Koyoharu Gotouge, Aya Yajima. All rights reserved. First published in Japan in 2019 by SHUEISHA Inc., Tokyo. English translation rights arranged by SHUEISHA Inc.

Printed in the U.S.A.

Published by VIZ Media, LLC
P.O. Box 77010
San Francisco, CA 94107

Library of Congress Cataloging-in-Publication Data

Names: Yajima, Aya, author. | Gotoge, Koyoharu, 1988- illustrator. | Allen, Jocelyne, 1974- translator.
Title: Demon slayer: kimetsu no yaiba : the flower of happiness / Koyoharu Gotouge, Yajima ; translated by Jocelyne Allen.
Other titles: Kimetsu no yaiba. English
Description: San Francisco : VIZ Media, 2022. | Series: Demon slayer: kimetsu no yaiba novels | Summary: "A mystical flower offers a prosperous future for its bearer. Determined to find the flower for Nezuko, Tanjiro makes a harrowing journey up a mountain. Revisit the Demon Slayer Corps with five tales of love, friendship, and courage!"-- Provided by publisher.
Identifiers: LCCN 2022013441 (print) | LCCN 2022013442 (ebook) | ISBN 9781974732524 (paperback) | ISBN 9781974735426 (ebook)
Subjects: CYAC: Short stories. | Fantasy. | LCGFT: Short stories. | Fantasy fiction. | Light novels.
Classification: LCC PZ7.1.Y34 De 2022 (print) | LCC PZ7.1.Y34 (ebook) | DDC [Fic]--dc23
LC record available at https://lccn.loc.gov/2022013441
LC ebook record available at https://lccn.loc.gov/2022013442

viz.com

10 9 8 7 6 5 4 3 2 1
First printing, October 2022

CONTENTS

DEMON SLAYER
KIMETSU NO YAIBA
The FLOWER OF HAPPINESS

TANJIRO KAMADO

A kind boy who saved his sister when the rest of his family was killed. Now he seeks revenge. He can smell the scent of demons and his opponents' weaknesses.

NEZUKO KAMADO

Tanjiro's younger sister. When a demon attacked her, she turned into a demon. Unlike other demons, she tries to protect Tanjiro.

STORY

In Taisho-era Japan, the demons that the original demon, Muzan Kibutsuji, proliferated for over a thousand years have been eating people and threatening their happiness. Cursed because they produced Kibutsuji, the Ubuyashiki family devote themselves to defeating Kibutsuji—the root of all this evil—in order to atone. These human demon hunters—later called the Demon Slayer Corps—go up against the demons with blades called Nichirin Swords.

Demons have astounding power to heal themselves, but Demon Slayers take injuries in battle—they sometimes lose an arm or a leg, and can die. Even so, Demon Slayers stand up to the demons. Through it all, they must protect humans without fail.

ZENITSU AGATSUMA

He went through Final Selection at the same time as Tanjiro. He's usually cowardly, but when he falls asleep, his true power emerges.

INOSUKE HASHIBIRA

He went through Final Selection at the same time as Tanjiro. He wears the pelt of a wild boar and is very belligerent.

KANAO TSUYURI

Successor to Shinobu. She doesn't talk much and has difficulty making any decision by herself.

AOI KANZAKI

Member of the Demon Slayer Corps. She is in charge of treating and training Demon Slayers at the Butterfly Mansion.

SHINOBU KOCHO

A Hashira in the Demon Slayer Corps. Familiar with pharmacology, she is a swordswoman who has created a poison that kills demons.

Chapter 1
THE FLOWER
OF HAPPINESS

The crisp black kimono with long sleeves and beautiful patterns would illuminate his little sister's pale skin; the gorgeous golden-orchid *obi* belt might have made her, a natural worrier, frown and say it was too extravagant. Would she shed tears beneath her ebony hair tied up with ornaments in the elaborate *bunkin-shimada* style? Tears not of sadness, but of great joy.

My little sister, kinder than anyone in this world. A girl who hasn't lost the warmth she had as a person, even now, as a demon. I pray I can make you happy, the happiest girl in the world.

"A celebration?" he asked.

"Yes," Hisa said, and her eyes, already narrow as threads, narrowed even further with her broad smile. "Happily, one of the village's girls is to wed."

A family crest adorned with a wisteria flower was proof that the household would spare no effort in the service of the Demon Slayer Corps, all free of charge. Members of such families never forgot their debt to members of this corps for

saving them, and so they repaid them for their services. Thus, Demon Slayers injured in the line of duty sought out families with the wisteria crest.

Hisa's was just one such home.

That day marked ten days since Tanjiro, Zenitsu, Inosuke, and Nezuko had arrived at the house to rest and heal after a difficult fight. The demon Nezuko slept in a box of Kirikumo Cedar during the day, and the people of the household generally only had contact with the three boys. Thanks to meals bursting with all the mountain's bounty, fluffy futons, soft kimono, and heartfelt hospitality, the three of them and their broken ribs were recovering quite happily.

"She'll be leaving us for the home of a prominent man in the town closest to our village," Hisa told them.

"That is definitely worth a celebration. Congratulations to her," Tanjiro said from the bottom of his heart.

Hisa grinned and continued. "If you don't mind, I'd love it if you Demon Slayers were to celebrate with us."

"What? Us?"

"Of course," Hisa said. "That is, if you're well enough to join us. I'd hate for you to try to do too much too soon."

"No, no, we're all fine now." Tanjiro hesitated. "But are you really sure it's all right for us to go?"

Hisa nodded, a cloud of white hair bobbing on her head. According to her, there was to be an informal celebration with friends and family in the village that evening, and then the bride would make her formal departure the following afternoon. She would head to the neighboring town, where there would be a big ceremony at her new husband's house.

Any girl on the eve of her marriage was even lovelier than usual, her features full of hope, and this unusually good match had the villagers all the more excited.

"Everyone would be delighted if the Demon Slayers celebrated this joy with us," Hisa said.

"In that case, we happily accept." Tanjiro looked over his shoulder. "Right, Zenitsu? Inosuke?"

"Yeah, su—I mean, of course," Zenitsu responded, rubbing his hands together. "Unlike a demon hunt, there's absolutely nothing scary about a celebration like this. We'll get to eat delicious food and have a look at the beautiful young bride, so it's two birds with one stone. Er, but no matter how cute she is, she'll never be a match for Nezuko, you know? No, I know that. At any rate, I'm quite devoted to Nezuko. Please don't make any mistake about that."

"What's a celebration?" Inosuke, on the other hand, headbutted Tanjiro's side as he chomped away on the *manju* bun he held in both hands.

Ow…

Tanjiro frowned.

It was disturbing. Or rather, *Zenitsu* was disturbing.

This kind of thing was now—or rather, had become over the last few days—a thoroughly established ritual. The second Zenitsu found out that Nezuko was Tanjiro's little sister, his attitude had become excessively ingratiating.

With Inosuke, it was the headbutt. He likely just wanted to interact with people in his own special way, but he whipped out this headbutt whenever and wherever he got the chance. Honestly, it exhausted Tanjiro. His ribs would never heal with this going on.

And it was disturbing. *Zenitsu* was disturbing.

"Why do you say such creepy things, Zenitsu? Quit speaking so rudely of the bride. And you, Inosuke. This celebration is to honor the couple getting married. Ow! Inosuke, behave. Stop headbutting me."

He complained to his friends, gently, and turned back to Hisa, bowing before her.

"We would be delighted to join the celebration. Thank you so much."

"Well then, I am also delighted." The elderly woman lowered her head so far that her forehead nearly touched the tatami mat covering the floor. "Tonight, let us feast at the house."

A broad smile spread across her face.

"I expect that you young people would prefer meat, of course. Unfortunately, we poor villagers are not so familiar with such fashionable dishes."

"No, you've done so much for us already!" Tanjiro hurriedly waved his hands in protest and received an abrupt shove.

"That!" Inosuke shouted. "The thing you always make! Make that, lady! It's gotta be that!"

"Come on! Inosuke!" Tanjiro chided him.

"All you're saying is 'that.' You have to actually say what it is," Zenitsu snapped.

However, Hisa nodded in understanding. "You wish to have *that*, then. Tempura, yes? With the little coat?"

"Yaah!"

"Yes, yes," she reassured him. "We'll fry up a great deal of that. Do you have enough tea cakes?"

"No!" Inosuke barked. "So go and bring the thing! Got it? That thing!"

"Yes, yes. Mochi chips, hm? I'll bring some right away," Hisa responded. Unperturbed, she left the room.

It probably also had to do with her age, but Hisa's manner and bearing were very quiet. She made almost no noise. Once again, she slid the *fusama* door shut without a sound.

"Amazing that she even understood all the 'that.' He basically didn't say anything else." Zenitsu turned half-admiring, half-exasperated eyes toward the door Hisa had disappeared through.

"True," Tanjiro agreed.

Inosuke himself was intent on eating his manju and not paying attention to a word either of them said.

He had made a real fuss at the beginning of their stay. "Ain't no way! Wearing kimono, living inside a house, that's straight-up torture! Not a chance! Who do you think I am?! I'm the king of the mountain!!" But now, although his torso was still as naked as always, Inosuke appeared to have gotten quite comfortable with life indoors. At the very least, he didn't seem to think it was torture anymore.

From the moment they had first arrived on her doorstep, Hisa hadn't been afraid of Inosuke. The old woman had taken painstaking care of him, seeing to his every need as if he were her own grandson. The ostentatious boar's head never seemed to frighten her, and she paid no mind to any of the many strange things he did.

Thinking about this, Tanjiro was filled with a warm feeling. *I'm so lucky*, he thought.

He felt like he and his fellow Demon Slayers had grown closer over these past ten days, despite Zenitsu's weird fawning and Inosuke's constant and unpredictable headbutts. Perhaps it was because they had bathed and eaten the same meals together, or that they'd shared the same clean sleeping space, warm bathroom, and Hisa's heartfelt welcome.

Above all else, neither of them shunned Nezuko for being a demon. They welcomed her into their group just as she was. He couldn't begin to express how happy that made him.

"Hey! How can you just sit there and eat all the manju?!" Zenitsu cried, interrupting Tanjiro's fond contemplation. "Some of those are for me and Tanjiro, you know?! You stupid pig!"

"Shut up, Buttnitsu!" Inosuke barked. "You snooze, you lose!"

"It's *Zenitsu*! Who is Buttnitsu?!"

"Shut it, brat! This is my turf!"

"Ohh. I see. I'm so sorry. It's just, wait, what turf—gaaaah!"

"Crybaby! You'll never get the jump on me! Grah ha ha ha ha!"

Inosuke punched Zenitsu in the face, and the yellow-haired boy writhed on the tatami. Inosuke's throaty, bestial laughter filled the room.

Tanjiro let out a sigh. "Inosuke. You can't go punching Zenitsu."

Zenitsu got a proper jab in at Inosuke, and the boar-headed boy pummeled him mercilessly in return. Reluctant, Tanjiro stepped between them.

This, too, was becoming an established ritual.

"Aah, the bride was soooo beautiful!" Zenitsu sighed happily.
"Serious feast. Urp!" Inosuke burped.

As Tanjiro walked back to Hisa's with his friends after the banquet, he recalled how lovely and innocent the bride had looked. Blessed with good looks to begin with, the young woman dazzled with her beauty on the eve of her marriage into a powerful family.

The brilliant smile stretched across her face gave away the girl's happiness better than any words could have. The gorgeous black *furisode* kimono—patterned with flying cranes and blooming flowers—and the magnificent golden-orchid obi had paled in comparison to the wonder of that smile.

"So she…" he started to say.

"Who? What?" Zenitsu asked.

"Oh—it's nothing." Tanjiro shook his head slightly.

The bride could have been around Nezuko's age. The moment he had this thought, he felt a sharp pain in his heart.

Huh? Where'd that come from?

Frowning, Tanjiro gently shifted the wooden box on his back.

Skrtch skrtch.

He heard fingernails scratching from inside the box and nearly jumped up into the air.

Ah!

For some reason, his sister being awake when he'd thought she was asleep made his heart skip several beats.

"But why was that lady wearing that?" Inosuke asked no one in particular. "I mean, in a kimono with such long sleeves, she's not gonna be able to climb a tree. No way she's catching a rabbit or a bird." The boar head tilted to one side as if this were a true mystery for the ages.

"Aah-aah, this is exactly why I hate country bumpkins," Zenitsu said with a sigh. "She's not going to be living rough on the mountain, okay? That girl's going to be the wife of an important merchant. She's marrying into wealth. A rich man. Get it? She's a beauty, so she's going to marry a wealthy man, wear beautiful kimono, and spend her days cherished like a butterfly or a rare flower."

"Seriously, though," Inosuke continued. "Why pick a dark color like that? Doesn't she know the bees are gonna come right for her if she's wearing a black kimono up on the

mountain? I mean, come on. You gotta go for a color that's all *pow* for a party, y'know? So boring."

"I *told* you she's not going up into the mountains!" Zenitsu snapped. "The special black *furisode* kimono is just what a bride wears—that and the snow-white kimono. It's this way of saying, 'the only color I'll be dyed with is you' to her future husband. Aah, I wish someone would say that to me. Maybe even Nezuko... Wee hee hee!"

His voice slid up into a creepy falsetto as he trailed off ecstatically.

"*What* is this guy talking about?" Inosuke said blankly. "Total creep."

"Of all the people in the world, *you* don't get to say that!" Zenitsu flew into a rage at Inosuke's insult. "Right, Tanjiro?!"

"Huh?" Tanjiro jerked his head up and offered a noncommittal response. "Oh...I dunno."

His mind was strangely distracted and unsettled. He kept feeling something stuck in his throat.

"What's wrong? It's like you're somewhere else," Zenitsu said in an anxious tone, and he tugged on the sleeve of Tanjiro's *haori* coat. "Did something happen?"

"He's prob'ly hungry," Inosuke said, chewing on some mochi from the party. "You didn't eat anything back there, did you?

There was a whole mountain of delicious stuff too. Stupid."

He gulped down the last of the mochi and slammed a fist against his chest. "Hang on, Senjiro. I'll go back and get you the rest of that food!"

"Uh—no! You don't have to do that!" Finally snapping out of it, Tanjiro hurried to stop Inosuke's wild mission before it could start. He couldn't let him charge back into that celebration like some bandit. He'd ruin the happy day.

"Don't be shy. It's a boss's duty to take care of his underlings."

"I'm not being shy. I'm just not hungry."

"Don't eat when you can, and you'll regret it, y'know? There was a hunk of meat this big, okay?! A whole heap of fruit too!"

"I'm telling you, I'm really not hungry, Inosuke," Tanjiro insisted.

But Inosuke was like a dog with a bone, eventually forcing Tanjiro to bow deeply and beg Inosuke to not go back. Inosuke finally (albeit very grudgingly) gave up on his mission.

Zenitsu peered at Tanjiro's face, looking slightly concerned. "What's the matter, Tanjiro? You've been weird this whole time."

"Weird?" Tanjiro's eyebrows shot up. "Me?"

"Yeah. You're making, like, a weird sound."

A moment of silence passed, during which Tanjiro's heart skipped a beat. Zenitsu's sense of hearing was much sharper than that of the average person, and he could even pick out the "sounds" of different emotions. It worked a lot like Tanjiro's own sense of smell.

And now he was saying that Tanjiro sounded weird. Flustered, Tanjiro remained silent.

"I get it," Zenitsu murmured, preempting any explanation from Tanjiro with an unusually serious expression on his face. "It's about Nezuko, right?"

"Uh—"

Tanjiro's heart jumped up into his throat. When Tanjiro was at a loss for words, Zenitsu nodded to himself with a look that said he understood everything.

"You were picturing the day when Nezuko gets married, and you got all sad, didn't you?"

Tanjiro stared at Zenitsu, dumbfounded. "Huh?"

"Listen, Tanjiro. You can't be like that. For Nezuko's sake, just be happy for her when someone comes along to marry her, okay?"

Tanjiro still could not muster a sound. Zenitsu's comments slightly missed the mark. In his mind, demon

Nezuko would get married like a normal girl and go off to be with her husband's family like a normal girl. Zenitsu's thinking wasn't too surprising since he had never been concerned that Nezuko was a demon.

Tanjiro was deeply grateful for his friend's mindset, but that wasn't quite what was troubling him. He had this feeling that there was something fundamentally, definitively different going on in his heart, but he didn't know what it was. It just felt bad, like a small bone lodged in his throat.

"Yeah. You're making, like, a weird sound."
"It's about Nezuko, right?"

Why had he jumped in such surprise at Zenitsu's harmless comments? Confused, he gently placed a hand over his heart.

Thmp...thmp... He felt it carving out its tiny rhythm and opened his ears, listening as hard as he could. Still, he couldn't hear this sound that Zenitsu was talking about.

Well, of course not. It's not like my ears are as sharp as his. What exactly was going on with him? Tanjiro frowned.

Unaware of the confusion Tanjiro was feeling, Zenitsu spoke brightly of the day Nezuko would marry, while Inosuke listed the foods they had eaten earlier that were most delicious. Just when the anxious gloom in his heart was starting to overwhelm Tanjiro, he heard a childish voice cry out.

"Listen, Akari! You obviously can't, okay? It'll be dark soon. You'll get eaten by demons."

"But I want to marry into a big house in town just like Toyo! I don't wanna work!" protested an even younger voice.

"I said no!"

"You big meanie! You're no fun! You're a stupid meanie!"

"What did you say?! Go ahead and say that one more time!"

Tanjiro looked over and saw two little girls arguing. One was around ten, and the other was maybe seven. Their faces—brows furrowed, cheeks puffed out—were surprisingly alike, so they were probably sisters.

"Like Toyo"… Does she mean the bride from the party?

Tanjiro walked toward them, and the younger girl grabbed on to the older girl's sleeve when she caught sight of him.

"What's the matter?" he asked, crouching down so as not to scare them. "What are you fighting about?"

The older girl glanced at him and replied with her own question. "Are you a Demon Slayer? You're staying at Mrs. Hisa's house."

"Uh-huh." He nodded. "I'm Tanjiro. Are you sisters?"

"Yes. I'm Akane," the older girl said. "This is my little sister Akari."

The shy Akari hid behind her sister. She then poked her face out to peek at Tanjiro before ducking back.

Tanjiro grinned at this very childlike gesture. *Rokuta used to be like that too.* Actually, Shigeru, Hanako, Takeo, and even Nezuko had all gone through a stage like this.

As he remembered those long-gone days, Tanjiro asked the sisters, "When you said 'Toyo,' did you mean the girl who's marrying the merchant in town?"

"Yes," Akane said.

"So, did you know?" Akari popped her face out again. "Toyo, she found a vine lantern."

"A vine lantern?" Tanjiro cocked his head to one side. He'd been raised in the mountains, but this was the first time he'd heard this term. "Is that a flower or something?"

"Uh-huh. It's a flower." Akari bobbed her head up and down and pointed to the nearby mountain with a small finger. "It grows up there. If you find one, you can marry *purple*."

"Purple?" he asked and then understood. "Oh, you mean marry *into* the purple."

"That's how come Toyo gets to go be the wife of a rich man," the little girl told him smugly.

"That's just a superstition." Akari frowned. "It's a village legend from a long time ago. 'Keep the flower that only blooms on the night of the new moon against your skin, and you will marry the person you love and live a life happier than all others.' Akari heard the aunties saying that Toyo made such a good match, she must have found a vine lantern."

"Oh, I get it." Tanjiro slapped a fist into his open palm. "And since tonight's the new moon…"

"Yes." Akane nodded, looking troubled. "She says she's going to go pick one. Even though I keep telling her it's not a real flower."

So that was why they were arguing.

Their argument was silly, but the falling evening was no joke. Once it got dark—as it soon would—the demons would start to come out. The older sister was right to worry.

Tanjiro peered at Akari, still glued to her sister's back, as he said, "But the mountains are dangerous at night, you know?"

"I'm already six years old," the girl with the bowl cut replied with a headstrong look on her face.

Tanjiro burst out laughing in his head, but he made sure the look on his face was extremely serious as he explained, "It's dangerous for grown-ups too."

"Because of the demons?" she asked.

"Mm-hmm." Tanjiro nodded.

"Hmm. Are demons scary?"

"Mm-hmm. Very scary," Tanjiro told her in a grave tone.

Akari seemed to think for a moment. "Okay," she said, apparently reluctant. "I won't go up the mountain."

Akane's sigh showed her relief. "Thank you so much. You've been a very big help." She bowed deeply and then yanked on her little sister's arm. "Come on. Let's go."

Tanjiro watched the two of them walk away.

"What's the matter, Tanjiro? Who were those girls?" Zenitsu asked as he trotted over with Inosuke right behind him. "They say something to you?"

"Yeah." Tanjiro relayed what the girls had just told him.

"Pft! Stupid. Just kids playing around." Inosuke wasn't even the slightest bit interested, but Zenitsu seemed fascinated.

"Whoooa, what an interesting flower," he murmured. "How great would it be to marry the person you love and be the happiest person in the world? Although, the marrying into wealth part, I think that's a bit of a stretch."

"It's nothing more than a legend, Zenitsu," Tanjiro reminded him, remembering the burning intensity of Zenitsu's desire to get married. This, after all, was the guy who had begged a girl he'd just met on the road to marry him, sobbing all the while. "Akane said it's not a real flower."

"Well, of course it's not," Zenitsu agreed. "But girls, well, they're easy prey for these kinds of fantastic legends about love."

"They are?" Tanjiro said.

"Oh yeah. They like spells and stuff too, right?" Zenitsu told him, confidently. "There's that whole 'he loves me, he loves me not' thing too. A flower that only blooms on the night of the new moon is exactly the sort of thing girls go wild for. Oh, hey! They say your wish will come true if you make it on the night of the new moon, so maybe that's where it comes from. In that case, just maybe, just *maybe*. I mean, there are a lot of legends that aren't total garbage. There might actually be a flower like that."

"You really know your stuff, huh, Zenitsu?" Tanjiro complimented his friend's surprisingly astute analysis.

"Oh you! Flattery'll get you nowhere!" Zenitsu chuckled creepily in embarrassment, his face turning red. "Wee hee hee hee!"

When Tanjiro really thought about it, Zenitsu probably only knew all of this because he had some vulgar ulterior motive like making conversation with girls, but it still duly impressed Tanjiro.

Huh. So girls like that kind of stuff, he thought, and then paused. *Nezuko too?* He smiled at the feel of the hard Kirikumo Cedar box pressing against his back. The charming figure of the bride-to-be Toyo overlapped with Nezuko in his mind. His little sister wearing the traditional, beautiful black kimono and smiling. Happily. Joyfully. This image quickly cleared away the fog in his head.

Was that it…? He finally understood the cause of his gloomy anxiety.

"Hey! You guys! Who cares about some dumb flower? We gotta get back to the old lady's! She's waiting to fry us some of that stuff with the little coat!" Inosuke yelled as his stomach loudly growled. Remembering the feast leftovers probably made him hungry. "C'mon! Quit dragging your feet!"

"Wait. You want to eat *again?* Does your stomach never get full?" Zenitsu said, rolling his eyes. He looked back at Tanjiro. "What's wrong? You coming?"

Tanjiro stood stock-still in the road, staring off into the distance.

"Tanjiro?" Zenitsu asked.

He hesitated slightly and then said, "Sorry. I have to do something first. You and Inosuke go on ahead."

Impatient, he turned and hurried after Akane and Akari.

"Oh… There they are!"

He'd been worried he would have trouble finding them given the time since they had walked away, but these were two little girls, after all. Aided by the power of his nose, Tanjiro quickly caught up with the small shadows happily holding hands in the twilight sun.

"Akane! Akari!" he called out. "Wait a second!"

Older and younger sister looked back at him with similarly curious looks on their faces.

"Mr. Demon Slayer?"

"Is something wrong?"

"I want you to tell me everything you know about the vine lantern," he said. The girls each blinked slowly, eyes opening wide in surprise.

"Wee hee hee… What? Really? Why, you… Wee hee hee! Fwoo fwoo… Huh? Hee hee hee hee… Oh, Nezuko, you… Ngh ngh…"

That evening, Zenitsu was in the middle of an extremely good dream when someone fiercely shook his shoulders where they poked out from under his blankets.

"Nooo... Go away... Aah, I'm at a really good part right now... Don't bother me, Inosuke... Ngh... Wee hee hee... That's not true... Mwah mwah... Nezuko, you are so cute... Snrr hee hee." He rolled over to try and escape the annoying hands on his shoulders.

The person trying to wake him remained silent but undeterred.

Now something whapped him on the forehead, and his brow creased as he slept.

"Mmm... What? Now it's Tanjiro? I'm talking about love with Nezuko, so hang back a bit... Fwoo fwoo... Right, Nezuko..."

Whap, whap, whap.

"Ever since we first met, Nezuko, I've been... Hee hee! Wee hee hee... No, it's true... Snrr... Right? We're destined to be together... Snrr snrr..."

Whap, whap, whap, whap, whap, whap, whap, whap!

"Gah! Come on! I said, shut up! What's with the whap-whap-whapping! Huh? What, exactly?! You're being mean! Why do you both hate me?" Zenitsu snapped, finally opening his eyes at the persistent slapping.

However, the person peering at him in the darkness was not Inosuke nor Tanjiro, but Nezuko, who was out of her box for some reason. The moment he saw her, his anger vanished without a trace.

"N-N-Nezuko? W-w-w-what's the matter? I mean, it's the dead of night." Zenitsu literally leaped up from his futon, flustered, his face as red as a lobster. "Wait. Did you actually come to see me?! No, of course that's not it. Ah, ah ha ha… Oh! Is Inosuke's snoring too loud maybe? Ha ha ha! He really is something else, huh?"

Nezuko shook her head firmly, and her glossy black hair swung back and forth.

"Huh? Th-that's not it? Wait. Me? Is it *me*? Was *I* snoring?! Or maybe I was grinding my teeth?! I'm so sorry!" Zenitsu flailed his hands pointlessly, rushing to apologize.

Nezuko shook her head once more as she indicated the futon next to him with an impatient "Mmf."

Here, the unnatural movement of Zenitsu's hands stopped. "Huh? What? Is something wrong with Tanjiro?"

Zenitsu peered at Tanjiro's futon, and his eyebrows jumped up as he shrieked in surprise. The futon where Tanjiro should have been sleeping was empty. Inosuke, meanwhile, was snoring on the futon on the opposite side, dead asleep.

Nezuko looked around anxiously. Zenitsu suddenly understood. She was looking for Tanjiro.

Most likely, Nezuko had climbed out of her box after night fell, realized her brother was nowhere to be found, and shaken Zenitsu awake.

Aah, dear, sweet Nezuko. You're too cute. You really do love your big brother. I'm so jealous, Tanjiro. But she came to me for help and not Inosuke. Aah, dear, sweet Nezuko, I love you.

Zenitsu's heart tightened in his chest.

"I'm sure he just went to the washroom," he said reassuringly, with a flirtatious look. "He'll probably be back soon."

"Mmf! Mmmf!" Nezuko shook her head fiercely, like she was angry. "Mmf!"

Sensing that something was out of the ordinary with her, Zenitsu flipped back Tanjiro's blanket and touched his futon.

"Huh?"

It was cold. The icy chill drained the red from Zenitsu's face. The total lack of warmth made it very hard to believe that someone had been sleeping there until recently.

When Zenitsu searched the room, he found that Tanjiro's corps uniform and his Nichirin sword were gone. In their place, the kimono he'd been wearing was set out, folded neatly.

"So he went somewhere? Tanjiro?!" Zenitsu was worried now. He yanked open the sliding door that led to the garden. It was dark outside, which made the stars shine all the more beautifully.

"Right," he said. "Today's the new moon."

The events of the afternoon suddenly came flooding back to him.

The way Tanjiro had sounded different from normal after seeing the young bride. The legend of the vine lantern, the flower that brings marriage to one's true love and all the happiness in the world. Tanjiro's heart skipping a beat the moment Nezuko's name came up. The wooden box shaking on his back as Tanjiro went after the two girls.

Zenitsu looked back at Nezuko. "He couldn't have."

The girl who Tanjiro loved more than anything in this world—certainly more than his own self—scowled and clutched her brother's futon.

His field of view showed the starry heavens.

"Unh… Unnnh…"

Tanjiro was lying on the damp ground.

The apparent cliff he'd fallen from was higher up than he'd expected. Thankfully, he'd happened to fall on a pile of dead leaves, which saved him, but it seemed that he'd lost consciousness for a while.

"Ngh!" A quiet groan slipped out of him when he tried to sit up.

His whole body hurt, especially his ribs. They had almost completely healed, and now this. He would feel incredibly pathetic if they broke again. And he'd never be able to look Hisa in the eyes again, not after she'd taken such good care of him.

I can't believe I fell off a cliff.

Ashamed by his own lack of training, he sat up as gently as he could. The dull pain remained, but it seemed that nothing was broken.

Just as he let out a sigh of relief, a nearby shrub rustled. The cause of his fall appeared from between its branches, and Tanjiro's face split into a grin.

"So you're okay? That's a relief."

A wild boar about the size of an adult human snorted and stared hard at Tanjiro.

"You be careful from now on, okay?" he said with a smile, and the boar snorted again.

A few moments earlier...

It was all fine and good to climb up the mountain in search of the vine lantern, but finding a flower in the middle of the night was a much tougher task than Tanjiro had expected. He might have been raised in the mountains, but this was not the mountain he'd grown up on. Walking along the unfamiliar paths—eyes open for a flower that might not even exist—required more perseverance than he'd thought.

Making it all the more difficult was that Akane and Akari had essentially zero artistic abilities, and the picture they had so painstakingly drawn for him was almost entirely useless.

"People say the leaves are a really clear, bright green. And the stem's got these big saw teeth."

"I heard the flower has five petals. They're all floofy like this. See? Look. This kind of shape. Mm-mm, not like that. No. Like this, I said. Here. Honestly, you're so bad at this."

"I guess most of the flowers are this really deep red. Soooometimes, there'll be regular red or white ones, though. Hmm, what else? Oh! I remember. I heard each petal's shaped like a wild boar's eye. And they're very cute. The smell? No one says anything about how they smell..."

Based on these few clues—the shape of the leaves, the number of petals, the color—Tanjiro had been looking along

the sides of the path when a boar poked its head out from the bushes.

The boar looked very much like Inosuke. Its breathing was ragged, and its entire body smelled of anger. Tanjiro looked and found a fresh wound at the base of one leg. It was pretty deep, which was probably why the creature was so worked up.

"Are you hurt? Here, let me take a look. It's okay... Aah, no. If you move like that, the cut will...! Watch out!"

When he tried to soothe the boar and get it to let him treat its wound, it very nearly fell from the cliff. Tanjiro threw himself after it to protect the animal with his own body.

And now here he was.

"There we go! You're all fixed up. You be careful from now on, okay?" Tanjiro grinned after the now-docile boar let him take care of its wound. The more he looked at it, the more it looked exactly like Inosuke.

"Okay, I have to go look for this vine lantern. You take care," Tanjiro said, and was about to leave when the boar clamped its jaw down on his jacket.

"Ah! What's wrong? You hungry? But this is a haori. It's not for eating."

"Hrrrrn!" The boar growled as it tugged on Tanjiro's haori.

"Huh? You want me to come with you?"

"Hrrrrrrn!"

"Okay. Got it."

Reading what was in the boar's heart, Tanjiro bobbed his head up and down. The boar trotted off confidently, so Tanjiro let himself be led. After they'd walked a fair distance, a small cave came into view beyond the dense foliage.

"Ah…"

To one side of the cave, a crimson flower bloomed. Tanjiro opened his eyes wide.

Clear, bright-green leaves… Each of the flower's five petals opening gently outward in the shape of a boar's eye…

"A…vine lantern?" Tanjiro gasped.

The lovely flower was damp with dew that shone like scattered stars.

When Tanjiro's family had been taken from him in a single night, how relieved he had been to find that at least Nezuko was still breathing! How happy he had been, how

that fact had kept him going. Maybe Nezuko had become a demon so that she could live on and keep her cowardly older brother from being all alone… When this thought occurred to him, he felt such love and compassion for his sister, he nearly burst into tears.

Nezuko, so extraordinarily patient ever since she was little. So kind I almost want to cry. I swear I won't let anyone take anything from you ever again. I'll never let anyone hurt you.

Your big brother is going to make you happy. All the happiness I couldn't bring to the others, I'll give to you.

"Huh? Everyone's awake?"

When Tanjiro returned to Hisa's house, he noticed a serious commotion in the room where he and the others were staying. Even though it was the dead of night, a lamp was lit, and the voices inside were loud enough to hear in the hallway.

"I *told* you, that idiot Tanjiro went looking for a flower on the mountain! Yes, th. mountain at night. Pretty dangerous if some demon shows up, right? We're going to look for him, so you come too. That's what I'm trying to say here."

"Huh? Why should Lord Inosuke go looking for Konjiro in the middle of the night? You're good on your own, yeah?"

"The mountains at night are scary! It's too scary to go alone!"

"Tch! Coward. And why would that idiot Tanjiro go up the mountain, anyway?"

"I *told* you! He went to look for a flower! Listen when people talk to you!"

"A flower? Why would that idiot Butaro go off and pick a flower? That guy's practically a girl."

"He probably heard the story of the vine lantern and wanted to give one to Nezuko. Stupid Tanjiro."

"Huh? This wine lamb, it some kind of food?"

"*Vine! Lantern!* Those village girls were talking about it this afternoon. You were there. You heard them, right, Inosuke? You were chomping away on mochi. Did you forget?"

"I remember the mochi. It was great."

"Idiot! You stupid idiot! No brain in *your* head!"

"What did you say?!"

They sure are calling me an idiot a whole lot. And the way Inosuke constantly gets my name wrong is really something.

Swallowing hard, Tanjiro tentatively slid open the door.

"I'm back."

Inside the room, Inosuke was holding Zenitsu up by the throat.

"Whoa! What are you doing?! Stop it, Inosuke!" Tanjiro hurried over to break them apart. "Let go of Zenitsu."

"Shut up, Butajiro! This guy's making fun of me! I'm not stopping till I knock him through the roof!"

"I keep telling you, it's against corps rules for members to fight! Let go of him right now!" Tanjiro barked. He somehow managed to separate the two.

"Tch!" Inosuke clicked his tongue.

"Unnh, Tanjiroooo." Zenitsu clung to him.

Tanjiro patted Zenitsu's head gently and asked, "Where's Nezuko? In the box?"

His sister poked her head out from inside his own blankets and gazed at them silently.

"Well, well. So that's where you were?" Tanjiro perked up.

He excitedly pulled out the flower he had tucked carefully away in the pocket of his uniform. It was just the slightest bit bent, but not wilted at all. He gently held out the shining beauty toward his little sister.

"I brought you this. It's a vine lantern."

Nezuko stared at the flower.

"With this, you'll be able to marry the person you love and be the happiest girl in the world," Tanjiro told her, grinning.

But no matter how long he held it out, his sister did not reach for it. He cocked his head to one side.

She seemed unhappy somehow. Maybe he had caused her to worry by disappearing like that. If that was the case, he had wronged her.

"Sorry for worrying you." His voice grew even gentler. "The flower's pretty, right?"

Nezuko looked at the flower silently, took it from his hand, and put it in her hair. Seeing Tanjiro break out into a grin, she smiled too. And then she took the flower from her hair and affixed it to his head.

"Hm? No, Nezuko, that's not what I meant," Tanjiro said. "I don't need the flower. You…"

The smile disappeared from her face, and her eyebrows rose up in concern.

Ah…

Her eyes looked incredibly sad. He felt like he'd seen that emotion in them somewhere before, a long time ago.

The younger sister stared at her older brother. As if reproaching him. He caught the scent of something like pity.

"Sorry…"

Unable to do much other than return her gaze, he abruptly remembered a moment from the past.

"Stop apologizing, Tanjiro. Why are you always saying you're sorry?"

Tanjiro gasped. He forgot why now, but his little sister had been angry for once that day. She had looked at her brother with a rare sternness.

It was—right, it had been a cold day. The falling snow was icy, enough to freeze him to his core.

He was pretty sure it had been not long after their father died.

"Is it because we were poor? Did you feel unworthy because you wore a tattered kimono?" his little sister said, glaring at her big brother. More than anger or annoyance, he could smell sadness.

"We tried as hard as we could, but it didn't work. It's no one's fault. Things don't go exactly the way we want them to. We're only human."

The Nezuko in his memory overlapped with the Nezuko of the present. His heart cracked at those eyes brimming with such deep sadness.

No.

No, that's not it, Nezuko.

I just… I wanted you to be happy.

"You get to decide where your happiness comes from. What's important is now.*"*

"Oh!"

When Nezuko's words came back to him, he suddenly felt like he'd been punched hard in the head.

Right.

His little sister had said that to him after he kept on apologizing because their family was poor. He couldn't dress her up in beautiful kimono, they did nothing but work day in and day out, their beloved father was dead, and Tanjiro was always asking his little brothers and sisters to be patient.

Stop apologizing, she'd said.

"I know you understand. You know how I feel."

Ohh...

Understanding dawned on him. He and Nezuko felt the same way.

Above all else, he wanted to make Nezuko human again. He wanted her to live the lavish life of a girl her age. He prayed she would do it alongside a boy she loved.

I want her to be the happiest girl in the world. There wasn't a day that went by that he didn't have this thought.

Yet, Nezuko felt exactly the same way. Just as Tanjiro held his sister in his heart, she held him in hers. That was why she had given him the flower that brings happiness.

Alive now, with a future ahead of her, Nezuko was not an unhappy girl. Their family had been slaughtered, she had been turned into a demon, and they would certainly come up against other hardships. But she had been accepted by the leader of the Demon Slayer Corps, she had friends who cared about her, and she even had a boy who loved her and cared not at all about her being a demon. Tanjiro himself was fighting for her happy future.

"Thanks, Nezuko." He pulled his sister to him and hugged her gently.

Nezuko responded by squeezing her brother tightly.

At this certain, warm pressure, tears spilled unbidden from his eyes, and for a while, he simply hugged her silently.

"Hey, why're you crying?" Inosuke asked curiously. "You hurt or something?"

"Inosuke," Zenitsu chided him quietly through his own tears as the moment's emotion swept through him. "Read the room. If you can't, then at least shut up."

"So?" the boy in the boar head replied. "Why'd Soichiro go traipsing around the mountain, anyway?"

"You—! Were you not listening to a word I said? He went up there to pick the vine lantern. See? That." Zenitsu pointed at the flower in Tanjiro's hair.

Inosuke glanced at the flower lazily and said casually, "But that's not a vine lantern."

"Huh?" Tanjiro and Zenitsu replied in perfect unison, gaping.

"It's, uh, too bad about yesterday, huh?" Zenitsu said timidly to Tanjiro the next morning. Tanjiro was absently lying in the yard and bathing in the sun.

In the center of the yard, Inosuke was racing around, shouting, "Boar super charge!"

Next to Tanjiro was the wooden box that held Nezuko.

The flower that Tanjiro had picked the night before turned out to be not a vine lantern, but a boar winterberry. Because the petals were terribly sweet, animals generally devoured them. For some reason, boars wouldn't touch them, and because of that, they bloomed quite often near boar dens.

In other words, the boar the previous night hadn't read Tanjiro's mind, but had simply invited him back to its den as thanks for saving its life and treating its wound.

This flower didn't only bloom on the night of the new moon, apparently. It also bloomed the night of the full moon and in the morning and afternoon, as one would expect from a flower.

"It's because I was saying all that stuff about making girls happy and that maybe the flower actually existed, huh? I feel kind of bad." Zenitsu hung his head.

"No, I decided to do this myself. It's not your fault at all." Tanjiro shook his head with a smile. "Yesterday, you said that I sounded weird, right?"

"Huh? O-oh, yeah, I did. And?"

"I didn't really get it myself at the time, but when I saw Toyo looking so happy, this beautiful bride, I thought how

miserable Nezuko must be not being able to bathe
in sunlight."

And then there was him, not being able to dress her in
beautiful kimono. Not being able to let her live in the light
of the sun. Dragging her into bloody battle, hurting her, not
being able to give her a single one of the joys of a girl her age.

He'd felt so bad about all of it, he could hardly stand it.
He hadn't known what to do.

"But Nezuko..."

Zenitsu looked back at him in silence.

Nezuko was not a girl to be pitied and assumed unhappy.
Just like she had when she was a person, she was trying to
live and be present in the moment. Nezuko was the one
who would decide what happiness looked like to her. Maybe
that meant marrying someone she loved and running away
together. Or maybe not.

Either way, it definitely wasn't something he could push
on her as her older brother. And yet he had jumped to the
conclusion that his little sister's "now" was unhappy and
pitiable, and tried to push his "happiness" on her.

"I need to defeat Muzan Kibutsuji and make Nezuko
human again as soon as possible," Tanjiro announced, facing
forward. "I have to avenge our family."

"Tanjiro," Zenitsu said, sniffling. "I'll do whatever I can to help. I'm super scared, though. And to be clear, I'm totally useless, weak, and I'm sure I'll die soon. I need you to not rely on me at all, but…I'll fight wherever I can, so…"

"Zenitsu…"

"I really need you not to count on me at all, though." He lacked confidence to the point where he felt the need to repeat his statement. Even so, his kindness made Tanjiro happy.

"Hey! You guys gotta run around until you puke blood too!" Inosuke shouted so loudly that it echoed not only through the courtyard but the entire town, abruptly shattering the tender moment. "We're gonna take down the demon boss to make my third underling human again, right? So we gotta get stronger! Don't sit there whining your life away! Stupidjiro!"

"Who's this third subordinate?! How dare you talk about Nezuko—" Zenitsu erupted in indignation.

"You're exactly right, Inosuke." Tanjiro laughed. How straightforward, how unwavering Inosuke could be, was truly dazzling. "We have to get stronger."

"Right?!" Inosuke cried.

"What are you talking about, Tanjiro?" Zenitsu said, exasperated. "You'll break your ribs again, you know? And just when they're finally almost healed. Why should we come

here to rest and then have to throw up blood? The whole thing is a terrible idea!"

"Come on, minions! Follow Lord Inosukeeeee!" Inosuke's ferocious roar drowned out Zenitsu's complaints.

Tanjiro heard the excited cry of a young villager on the wind. "The bridal procession's coming!"

He gently closed his eyes and saw the fresh and unsophisticated bride-to-be Toyo in his mind, Hisa's gentle smile, and Akane and Akari watching over them, eyes glittering, cheeks flushed.

He stroked the wooden box next to him with one hand, and a sound came from inside, as if in response. A small, very gentle sound.

Smiling, he looked up at the deep blue sky.

It was a perfectly clear day, not a cloud to be seen.

Chapter 2
FOR WHOM

"Nezuko, watch your step."

There was a small bump on the ground ahead of them. Zenitsu held out his hand, and Nezuko gripped it tightly, without a word.

Whoa! Her hand is so soft. I'm holding hands with Nezuko right now! We're holding haaands! Yahooooo! Utterly lovestruck with the feeling of her supple skin against his, Zenitsu savored the joy rising in him.

After all his strict training in Total Concentration: Constant during the day, enjoying a nighttime walk with Nezuko during the brief period when the moon came out was his happiest hour. He had gotten permission from both Nezuko's older brother, Tanjiro, and the master of the mansion, Shinobu, so they could go out without the need for secrecy; they had nothing to hide.

At times like this, everything in the world seemed to shine. Even the crescent moon hanging in the night sky celebrated them.

"There's a field up ahead with tons of flowers, okay? You're not tired? Oh! There's loads of white clover. I'll make you a crown of flowers," Zenitsu said, a rush of blood reddening his cheeks.

Nezuko looked up at him with the bamboo gag across her mouth, pushed her perfect chin forward, and nodded firmly.

Zenitsu practically melted at this adorable gesture.

*Aaah, what a joy it is to be alive. I'm so glad I didn't get
turned into a spider that time!*

"See, Nezuko? Look!" he cried. "We're here! This is it!"

"Mn!"

Nezuko's face lit up when they arrived at the meadow not far
from the Butterfly Mansion. The field and its many flowers even
entranced a boy like Zenitsu. The scene enraptured Nezuko,
being a girl of that age, all the more. She looked around happily
in the pale moonlight, and a smile crept over Zenitsu's face as
he began to pluck the promised white clover. He would pick as
many as he could to make her a crown of flowers.

This has always been the only thing I'm really good at. How
lovely a flower crown would look against Nezuko's glossy
black hair! *I'll do one of just white clover, and then I'll make one
with all kinds of flowers. That way, it'll be gorgeous and colorful.*

"Hey, Nezuko? Which flower is your fav—" he started
and then stopped, leaving Nezuko to ponder what he'd been
about to say.

The moment he spotted a yellow flower blooming quietly
to one side of the clover, a faded memory sprang to vivid life
in his mind.

That flower...

"All right! I managed to slip away from Gramps." Zenitsu sighed in relief as he hid behind a large tree, watchful of his surroundings. "He's probably angry."

He felt the teensiest bit of guilt, but he couldn't do this anymore. Seriously, he would die.

His trainer Jigoro Kuwajima was old, but he was still full of vim and vigor. He had a habit of saying, "This isn't going to kill you!" Zenitsu was pretty sure it would, though. This time, he wouldn't just get hit by lightning and emerge with golden hair.

Sorry, Gramps, but this is all that I am. I'm nothing special. Forget about me—well, I don't actually want you to do that. Maybe you could just think of me from time to time—I really am sorry. I do love you, Gramps. I just can't take any more.

Zenitsu apologized to his teacher silently and hurried onward so that he could make it out of the mountains before

the already-low sun went all the way down. The first thing he'd do when he got into town was eat a delicious manju. Then he would have his fill of the girls walking to and fro along the roads.

No secret practice in the middle of the night today. He would actually sleep for the first time in a long time. Maybe he would even watch a moving picture.

Zenitsu's feet were light as he walked ever downward while imagining the evening that awaited him…but his feet stopped when he neared the foot of the mountain.

His extremely sharp ears had picked up a girl's pained sobs.

"This is bad! A girl is crying!"

Instantly he took on a heroic look, as if he were a totally different person. He parted the trees, leaped over rivers, raced down cliffs, and charged toward the source of the crying. At the end of this sprint, he found a girl in a snowy-white kimono kneeling in the grass and weeping.

"Hey! Are you okay?!" he called out to her. "Are you sick?"

"Eep!" The girl jumped. Then, ever so timidly, she looked over her shoulder. When she saw Zenitsu, she slumped in relief and started to cry again. "Unh! Unh! Unh…"

"S-sorry! I scared you, didn't I? Hey, you—are you really okay? Are you hurt someplace?" he asked earnestly, and the girl finally lifted her face.

By chance, their eyes met.

Her long feathery eyelashes glistened with tears. Her face would have put a flower to shame with its loveliness.

Aaaunh!

Feeling like he'd been shot through the heart, Zenitsu pressed a hand to the left side of his chest. Naturally, it was an arrow of love. Perhaps because he had lived without parents and never known the warmth of a family, he longed for love and marriage twice as much as the average person. He fell head over heels frighteningly easily.

Zenitsu was already in love with the girl weeping on the grass before him. He started to panic. All he wanted was to stop those tears somehow.

"Uh, um," he stammered. "I-if you don't mind telling me, why are you crying? I might be able to help!"

The girl said nothing and continued to weep.

"I'm Zenitsu Agatsuma. I've been studying swordsmanship with an old man way up high on this mountain," Zenitsu explained, trying to quell her unease at not knowing the first thing about him.

"Swords…manship?"

To Zenitsu, the "sound" of the girl shifted slightly, like she was anticipating something. He could hear in her a

faint hope emerging from a place where despair prevailed. Becoming that hope for this girl delighted Zenitsu.

"Okay. You can just tell me whatever you can tell me."

The girl finally stopped crying.

"My name is Sayuri," she told him in a trembling voice. "I live with my mother, stepfather, and two stepsisters in a small village up ahead. It's protected by wisteria flowers."

"Oh, you do? Sayuri, hm? What a sweet name." Thrilled to know the lovely girl's name at last, Zenitsu wriggled in place. "So, why'd you come up the mountain today, and in such a kimono? It looks hard to walk in."

"The truth is…" The girl's eyebrows dropped sadly. "One evening a few days ago, my stepfather encountered a demon here. He barely managed to escape by promising to send his daughter to take his place."

"Whaaat?!" Zenitsu cried. "A demon? You? How could he do that?! That's awful! That's so awful!"

"He had no choice. My mother and my stepsisters couldn't live without my stepfather." She lowered her eyes, and the tears clinging to her eyelashes plopped onto her cheeks. She said no more.

The black hair tied back high on her head was indescribably beautiful. Heedless of the consequences, her unbearable loveliness spurred Zenitsu to shout, "I—!"

"I'll go to the demon in your place, Sayuri, and take care of it lickety-split! You just wait at the foot of the mountain!"

As he walked along the dark mountain path, Zenitsu already regretted blurting that out. He'd put on Sayuri's kimono to complete the deception, and he kept tripping over the uselessly long sleeves. The sword hidden on his back made the outfit even harder to move in.

On top of it all, he was so scared of facing the demon, he could hardly stand it. *Wait. It's totally hopeless, right? I mean, taking down a demon all by myself? And what was that "lickety-split" part? Lickety-split?! There's no way I can do this.*

Maybe I could go slinking back to Gramps and get him to come with me. No, I don't have the time for that. Aaah, I'm going to die. I am definitely going to die.

Zenitsu moaned and groaned to himself. He wanted to bawl pathetically and run away that very moment, or sooner if possible. Still, he knew he was the only one who could halt the tears of that lovely girl. *Sayuri… She was super happy too.*

She had shed tears of anxiety and relief when Zenitsu said he would take care of the demon. The bright sound

of hope and joy in her grew louder, but he could also hear clear sounds of regret, apology, and…confusion. It was an extremely complicated and painful sound. Most likely, she had qualms about sending Zenitsu, a total stranger, into this dangerous situation.

She's such a nice girl.

He remembered the trembling sound she'd made as she had gripped his hands and told him to be careful before they parted. Not once did she blame her stepfather for immediately offering her up as a sacrifice because she wasn't related to him. Nor did she hold it against her mother for not trying to stop him. It was precisely because she had such a kind heart that Zenitsu sincerely wanted to help.

Even his burning love for the girl and his sense of chivalry couldn't overcome his intense fear of the demon. Heading toward the meeting spot the demon had given the stepfather, Zenitsu nearly ran off a thousand times. Each time, he managed to stop himself somehow.

A slender crescent moon hung in the night sky. He looked up at it through the breaks in the trees and prayed, "Please let it be a tiny, weak demon!"

He heard the sound of the demon.

"Eeep!" He clamped his hands over the scream that threatened to slip out of his mouth.

The demon sounded like lips being licked, waiting for a beautiful girl to come along so they could eat her tender flesh. A greedy, inhuman sound.

With his whole body shaking, and unable to utter a word, Zenitsu came to a stop. He absolutely couldn't make himself go any farther. No matter how he tried, he couldn't take another step.

As Zenitsu held his breath and stood immobile on the dark mountain, an enormous demon stepped out of the brush. Even with a quick glance, Zenitsu could tell that this was no person. The demon had an enormous arm growing out of its back, and each of its three hands held an enormous sickle. A large mouth stretched from ear to ear while six small, merciless eyes glimmered with darkness.

Oh no. This is it. I'm dead. Sayuri...I'm sorry.

Zenitsu's teeth chattered harder than ever as he stared up at this terrifying and massive creature, tall enough that it looked like it was touching the clouds.

Haah, haah, haah! Haah, haah, haah! Haah, haah, haah! Haah, haah, haah! His breathing was wild like that of a virgin maiden.

"You're the old man's youngest daughter?" the demon asked in a gravelly voice.

Zenitsu's heart nearly pounded right out of his chest.

"Y... Y-y-y-y-y-yes!" he barely managed to squeak out. He couldn't stop his voice from jumping up unnaturally. "M-m-my name is Zeniko."

The demon glanced at Zenitsu. "So, the old man went and lied to me to save his own skin. Exactly how is this ugly girl the village's greatest beauty?" It clicked its tongue in annoyance.

To take Sayuri's place, Zenitsu had yanked his hair back and painted his lips red with the juice of crushed flower petals, but he was still just a boy dressed up as a girl.

More than a few demons preferred the flesh of beautiful maidens, and Zenitsu supposed that this demon also possessed this particular proclivity. Its disappointment and annoyance at dashed expectations reached Zenitsu loud and clear, and he trembled in fear.

"Well, fine. I'll tear you apart and eat you. And then once the season changes and those hateful wisteria flowers wither and die, I'll go and eat the old man's other daughters and his wife right in front of him," the demon announced, wiping away the drool dripping from his mouth, seemingly toying with Zenitsu. "Punishment for taking a great demon like me for a fool."

Zenitsu could hear vicious delight. A cold sound without a hint of warmth, hungry for blood.

"First, I'll gouge out those eyes with the tip of this sickle. Next, your tongue," the demon muttered, licking its lips. "After that—"

"Eeegaaaaah...."

In his extreme terror, Zenitsu finally let go of reason.

He heard a thread snap in his head, and then the void swallowed him up.

"Hngah?!"

Zenitsu woke to the sound of something hitting the ground and whirled around. He noticed the demon's head lying at his own feet.

"Aaaaaaaaaaah!!" His scream echoed through the night on the mountain.

When he leaped back from the spot, he accidentally kicked the demon head, and it rolled away with a disturbing sound. Blood spurted from the base of the neck.

"Eeeeeeee!! Noooooooooooo!"

The demon's six eyes were bloodshot and open wide, as if they had seen something unbelievable in its last moment. The place where the head had been severed from its body was perfectly level, as though a single stroke from a sharp blade had set the head free.

The demon's head was just sitting there now, like a big daikon radish.

"Wait, what, what?! Why is it dead? How? So suddenly?! I hate this! I haaaate this!" Zenitsu wailed. "How did its head get cut off? Why?! This is too scary! What is this? Why?!"

He understood nothing. Not the fact that the demon was suddenly in two pieces on the ground. Not the fact that he was for some reason holding the sword he'd hidden on his back. And not the fact that his snowy-white kimono was stained with droplets of the demon's blood.

"Did someone rescue me?" he cried. "Hey, where are you? Someone rescued me, right?!"

Weeping, he looked around, but there was no one else there.

Oh!

He had a sudden flash of insight. Only one person in this whole world would save a guy like him.

"Gramps..." Fresh tears filled Zenitsu's eyes.

Most likely, Jigoro had come to drag him back to that training hell and rescued him from the demon. Then he'd slipped away again, no doubt guessing that there were factors he wasn't aware of at play here.

Gratitude and contrition filled Zenitsu's heart.

"Thanks, Gramps," he whispered. "I promise I'll make Sayuri happy. Thanks for everything. And thanks...for helping a guy like me. You take care of yourself, okay?"

Still crying, Zenitsu sheathed his sword, bowed deeply toward the dark woods, and then left the area, looking like he had made his peace with the past. When he had disappeared into the darkness, a shadow carrying a cane moved with a rustling noise deep in the brush.

"Idiot apprentice," he choked out in a hushed voice. "I keep telling you, you've got talent no one can beat, but you just won't listen for some reason."

Sayuri was waiting. She was there up ahead, waiting for him! Lost in a dream, Zenitsu clutched a bunch of yellow lilies he'd picked along the way.

"Thank you...Zenitsu. I love them."

He saw Sayuri's happy face in his mind and chuckled creepily out of his own immense awkwardness.

He caught sight of someone clad in his kimono on the path ahead.

"Oh! Sayuri—" He started to wave and then stopped in his tracks.

She wasn't alone. A rustic young man stood next to her, looking toward Zenitsu with the same unease with which Zenitsu regarded him.

"Zenitsu..." Tears welled up in Sayuri's eyes.

Zenitsu froze. At that moment he understood everything. Sayuri had guessed that he felt more for her than just kindness or sympathy, which was why he'd volunteered to take her place.

But she was already in love with someone else.

That was the reason for the complicated and pained sound he'd heard her making. It wasn't that she had gone out of her way to deceive him. She simply hadn't said anything. She wanted to live—she didn't want to die—so she had clung to

whatever straw she could and held her tongue. Sayuri wasn't like the girl who had made Zenitsu give her money so she could run away with someone else.

He had clearly heard the sound she'd made. He'd just interpreted it in a way that worked for him. Even now, the sound was saying, *I'm sorry. I'm sorry.* Almost heartbroken.

It's not your fault, Sayuri.

Feeling his exultation cool, Zenitsu gave the girl a smile nonetheless. His heart throbbed painfully in his chest. "The demon's dead. You don't have to worry anymore."

"Th-thank you so much," she said quietly. "Thank you."

"Thank you so much!" the boy cried, practically prostrating himself before Zenitsu. "We will never forget this great debt! I'll take her away from that house and her awful stepfather. Thank you—so much, Lord Demon Slayer!"

Shut up! I didn't do all that for your sake! I did it for Sayuri! Although it was Gramps who actually defeated the demon, okay?! Dammit! It's even worse that he's not some half-wit brute and seems like a really good guy. Curses!

Zenitsu hid the lilies behind his back, weeping tears of blood inside.

"Zenitsu... I, um." Tears spilled from Sayuri's eyes. "I'm so sorry."

Zenitsu was too overwrought to respond to her heart-felt apology.

"I… I really am sorry."

The sound of her tormenting herself was agonizing.

"Sayuri. Be happy," he told her.

"I will." She bowed her head over and over again, crying all the while.

Finally, the couple returned to the village, leaning into each other.

Zenitsu watched them go with a smile.

"Sob! Sob!"

Once he was alone, the tears welled up in his eyes. Through blurred vision, he stared absently at the flowers he'd picked to give to Sayuri. The yellow lilies. In the language of flowers, they meant "cheer" and "falsehood."

Grah!

In his tortured state, he raised his arm to throw them down onto the mountain path. And then stopped. He fought to hold back his tears as he sensed someone nearby.

At some point, Jigoro had come to stand beside him. He made a strict and scary, but still gentle, sound.

"Um." Zenitsu nervously opened his mouth. "Gramps. I—"

"You idiot!" he barked, and Zenitsu flinched. "How many times have I *told* you, and yet here you run off from training again? And why are you dressed like this? There's ugly, and then there's *ugly!*"

"Eeep! I'm sorry!"

"Honestly! Having a fool for an apprentice is taking years off my life," Jigoro muttered with a sigh.

With nowhere else to go, Zenitsu shrank into himself.

"But you're no ordinary fool," the older man continued.

"What…"

"You're a massive fool."

Zenitsu clammed up and grew even smaller, while Jigoro's voice grew just the slightest bit softer.

"You're a massive, kind fool, you are."

"Gramps."

Zenitsu lifted his face in surprise, and Jigoro placed his hand on Zenitsu's head. It was a large, rough hand. The hand of a former Hashira that had annihilated demons and saved many people. This was the sort of hand Zenitsu had always dreamed of having. The strong and kind hand of a man he looked up to.

"You didn't turn your back on that girl," Jigoro said. "You didn't give in to your fear. You fought well."

"You were the one who saved me, Gramps," Zenitsu said dejectedly. "I was too scared to do anything."

"What is *wrong* with you?" Jigoro asked, exasperation in his voice. "You think *I* defeated that demon?"

"Huh? I mean, didn't you? While I was unconscious, you—"

"You're the one who killed it, Zenitsu."

"What?" Zenitsu looked bewildered, unable to process the words coming out of his teacher's mouth.

Huh? What's that mean? Gramps defeated that demon. Why's he saying I did? Huuuh? Zenitsu's world turned upside down for a moment, but he then realized Jigoro was probably talking about Zenitsu's spirit.

I didn't run away from the demon, so Gramps rescued me. He's saying that's the same as if I killed it myself. Is that it? That's definitely what he's trying to say, right? I mean, Gramps. He skips over all the details. It's hard to get what he's even saying. After convincing himself that this had to be the truth, he nodded in agreement.

"Zenitsu," Jigoro said to his apprentice. "You know what makes a good swordsman?"

"Huh? Being strong, of course. Like you, Gramps," Zenitsu replied immediately, and Jigoro flushed just a little.

He cleared his throat. "So then, what do you think you need to be strong?"

"Huh? I… I mean," Zenitsu stammered.

"Kindness," Jigoro announced meaningfully. "Kindness makes a person's heart tougher than nails, tougher than anything. A sword swung for the sake of someone else is the strongest sword in this world. That's what you need."

The old teacher's eyes, which normally only raged at him, were unfathomably kind now as they settled on this unworthy apprentice.

"No matter what else is going on, you turn your heart toward the weak and be their shield. It's because you know weakness yourself that you can do this."

Zenitsu's throat and eyes were suddenly hot, and the inside of his nose throbbed, leaving him unable to respond.

"So long as you don't lose that kindness, you're bound to become a great warrior."

"Gramps…" Tears spilled from his eyes. "I… I…"

Zenitsu sobbed, and Jigoro gently stroked his yellow hair in silence.

That day, too, a crescent moon had sat in the sky above them.

Sayuri, I hope you're doing well.

Zenitsu narrowed his eyes happily as he looked out at the yellow flowers swaying in the breeze. He felt a slight tugging on his sleeve and looked down to find Nezuko's unhappy face. That brought him back to himself.

"Oh, sorry, Nezuko!" he cried. "I'll make that crown right now, okay?"

"Mmf!"

"To apologize for getting distracted, I'll make you the most beautiful flower crown, okay?" he said, cheerfully. "I know. How about we make one for your brother and that idiot Inosuke too?"

Nezuko smiled happily. "Unh!"

"Ha ha ha!"

Her smile made Zenitsu smile too. He was certain that Sayuri was living happily ever after somewhere with that kind boy of hers.

Zenitsu was a far cry from the strong swordsman Gramps had told him about that day. He was a weak crybaby, scared of everything, and he ran away all the time. To be honest, he didn't know whether or not he was even kind.

But someday… For sure.

Vowing this in his heart, the boy plucked the most beautiful flowers in the field for his darling girl.

Chapter 3
**CHRONICLE OF A
FORTUNE-TELLING FUSS**

"I see trouble with women in your future."

"Huh…?" Tanjiro stopped in his tracks at the ominous voice he heard above the hustle and bustle of the city.

Zenitsu and Inosuke came to stand beside him.

He whirled his head around in search of the voice's owner and spotted a small, elderly woman in the crossroads. She was clad in a lavender kimono and covered in wrinkles, with a head of magnificent white hair.

Tanjiro turned questioning eyes on her.

The old woman shook her head slightly. "Not you," she said curtly.

Tanjiro looked toward Inosuke.

"Not that pig head either. The fellow with the yellow hair there."

"Huh?" Zenitsu, oblivious to the proceedings up to that point, looked shocked and pointed at himself. "What? Y-you can't mean me?"

"Mm." The woman nodded wearily.

"Ma'am, what do you mean, 'trouble with women'?" Tanjiro asked.

"I mean the disaster that befalls a man because a woman finds him favorable," the woman replied in a solemn tone. "I can see that fortune on the young man's face."

"What are you talking about, old hag?" Inosuke snorted. "You not in your right mind?"

"Inosuke!" Tanjiro chided him.

"Insolent child! I'm not an old hag!" the old woman roared.

Tanjiro and Zenitsu jumped the tiniest bit, but Inosuke was indifferent to her anger.

"So old geezer, then?" he said. "Guess it doesn't much matter. Old is old."

"I'm telling you for your own good." The old woman had apparently decided to ignore Inosuke. She stared hard into Zenitsu's eyes, boring holes into them, and sternly ordered, "Don't go near any ladies today. Avoid them to every extent you can. If possible, it's best not to even *speak* with one."

"That's just ridiculous." Zenitsu smiled knowingly at Tanjiro. That smile froze on his face, however, at what the old woman said next.

"You will die," she intoned.

"Ngah?!"

"If a lady starts to think kindly toward you, make no mistake, you will die—and in the most horrible way you can imagine. I pray you bear that in mind." The old woman dug around in the deep sleeves of her kimono. She retrieved a beat-up paper charm. The characters written on the yellowed, torn scrap were essentially impossible to decipher.

"Won't do much besides give your heart some peace, but take it."

She pushed the charm into Zenitsu's hand and walked away. She didn't even press the boys for some outrageous sum as payment for the fortune or the charm. That made the whole thing *more* disturbing.

Zenitsu froze. He stood rooted to the spot as though his soul had fled his body.

"Zenitsu?" Tanjiro asked timidly.

"Aaaaiiiiiieeeeeeee!" Zenitsu shrieked with a high-pitched, annoying nasal whine.

The unbearably ugly scream, like that of a stuck pig, echoed through the crowd.

"What, what, really... What the heck? Me *dying*? I mean, that's scaryyyyy." Zenitsu clutched Tanjiro's jacket as he completely lost his head, all kinds of fluids flowing freely down

his face. "And we were just about to go home… Why did she have to tell me I'll die? I don't get it! It doesn't make sense!"

"Zenitsu."

Tanjiro had an inkling of how his friend felt. Having completed their mission outside of town the previous night, they had rested at a nearby Wisteria House and were just buying some treats to bring back to the Butterfly Mansion.

"If you can, please pick up some cakes or something on your way back."

Shinobu Kocho, the master of the Butterfly Mansion, had made this request of them. She had perhaps been trying to give them a bit of a break, concerned that the three Demon Slayers had spent all their time training frantically ever since their mission on the Infinity Train.

This town was a rather large one, so everything they saw was new and strange. At first, Inosuke had hidden behind Tanjiro, frightened of the unfamiliar crowds, but he was soon chatting excitedly about everything that caught his eye.

"Hey! What's that?" "That horse is hauling a huge box!" "Why are they dressed so weird?" "Doesn't something smell real good? Is it that one with the little coat?!"

Zenitsu, the only one of them accustomed to the city, looked exasperated—"You're so embarrassing"—but he put real effort and interest into selecting what they should bring back for the girls at the mansion.

As they considered which snacks were often set out at the Butterfly Mansion, they went back and forth with each other. Not that, not this one either…

Eventually, they settled on the safe choice of manju. At a shop popular with women they purchased enough of the tasty buns for everyone, and had been just about to start out on the road home when the old woman proclaimed Zenitsu's sudden death sentence.

That would have thrown anyone into a panic.

"Nooooo… Why only me? Seriously, why? Come on, tell me! Aaauuuuugh!"

"Zenitsu, calm down."

Zenitsu crumpled into sobs, and Tanjiro tried to console him.

"Meep, meep, meep, meep. You're so loud," Inosuke said coldly. "A man doesn't shake in his boots. Ya gotta stand up and fight!"

"So mean!" Zenitsu opened his eyes wide in horror. "You're so mean, Inosuke! I mean, I knew that, basically. But still, this is too much, you know? I might die here, you know?! And she said it would be a really horrible death too!"

"Inosuke, just think a minute about how Zenitsu feels," Tanjiro interjected. He did actually feel bad for Zenitsu. "I

mean, anyone would be shocked and scared if they got told out of the blue they were about to die."

"Even from just some old hag's ravings?"

"She wasn't raving. She told his fortune."

"Same difference," Inosuke said flatly.

Thinking that Inosuke might not know what a fortune was, Tanjiro tried to teach him from scratch. "Listen, Inosuke. When we say fortune, we mean—"

"Like they say, fortune-telling's hit or miss," Inosuke cut him off. It appeared he was surprisingly versed in exactly what a fortune was.

Tanjiro opened his eyes wide in surprised admiration. "You really know your stuff, Inosuke."

"Well, y'know, I am the boss and all." Inosuke threw his chest out. "It's real rough having such sloppy minions."

Normally, Zenitsu would retort with something like "What are you the boss of, exactly?" or "I told you I'm not signing up to be your minion!" Instead, he simply pricked up his ears to listen and shook all over, looking like a cornered rabbit.

After thinking for a minute, Tanjiro nodded and turned to his friend. "Inosuke's actually right here, Zenitsu."

At the sound of his name, Zenitsu's shoulders jumped up. He silently turned frightened eyes on Tanjiro.

"There's not a fortune-teller in this world who always gets it right," Tanjiro said. "There's no way there could be."

If there existed such a person, then they would be a god. They wouldn't be human anymore. The frightening message had shaken more than just Zenitsu. Tanjiro had lost his head a bit too. But if they dealt with it as a fortune—nothing more, nothing less—then it was nothing to get unduly upset about.

"I...I guess so." Relief gradually spread across Zenitsu's face, and he sniffled loudly. "Now that you mention it, that granny seemed pretty dodgy, right? She's got to be a fraud—"

"There's a fortune-teller at the crossroads whose fortunes always come true?"

A woman's happy voice drifted toward them, as if to drown out Zenitsu.

"Wha?!" Zenitsu shuddered and ducked behind Tanjiro.

Tanjiro and Inosuke turned toward the voice to see a pair of young women dressed in showy kimono, chatting and laughing as they approached.

"Yes. The old woman with the white hair and lavender kimono."

"And she's really never wrong?"

"As far as I know. A friend of mine did what the woman told her, and she was engaged to a wonderful man two weeks later!"

"Aah, how delightful!"

"But I heard there are people who didn't do what she said and were seriously hurt."

"Goodness! How frightening!"

"You just have to follow her instructions, and you'll be fine."

"Oh dear! But there's no old lady in a lavender kimono here now."

"Goodness, you're right. I wonder where she went."

The girls, each adorable in her own way, looked around for the fortune-teller.

Zenitsu's eyes focused entirely on them, but his expression was devoid of its usual lechery. He was as pale as a ghost, his face stiff, a cold sweat on his forehead. Tanjiro noticed a curious clacking sound and wondered about it before realizing it was Zenitsu's teeth chattering.

This is bad...

"Zen—" Tanjiro started to caution him.

"Eeeeeaaaaaaaaaaaah!" The scream that escaped from Zenitsu's throat sounded like a chicken being strangled.

All eyes in the area immediately turned toward them. The two girls in question gave a little shout and dashed away as fast as they could.

"See! You hear that?!" Zenitsu yelped. "See! It's gonna come true! They said she's never wrong, didn't they?"

"Get ahold of yourself!" As Zenitsu threw his head back like a shrimp, Tanjiro held Zenitsu and slapped his cheek hard. He'd only meant to snap Zenitsu out of this fit, but he let out another scream.

"What? Why are you doing that?!"

"You have to calm down!" Tanjiro said.

"I can't! And also—ow!"

"Don't let a little fortune beat you, Zenitsu."

"It's no use! I mean, those girls said so! I'm going to die! I knew it. I'm going to die! Today! Wee hee hee hee!" He laughed creepily in his great terror.

Tanjiro was at a loss for what to do, and Inosuke broke his silence to click his tongue.

"Tch! Pathetic. Both of you underlings." The boar head leaned in closer. "C'mon. So now it's not just Monitsu, but Soichiro too? Did you not actually listen to what the old hag said?"

Tanjiro raised an eyebrow. "What do you mean, Inosuke?"

"This 'trouble with women,' means a guy gets in big trouble when a girl falls for him, yeah?"

"Yeah." Tanjiro nodded. "I'm pretty sure that's what she said." She had said that fortune was written on Zenitsu's face.

"You think anything like that's coming for this guy?"

Inosuke asked. Both Tanjiro and Zenitsu contemplated the assertion in stunned silence.

"Bunch of hooey," Inosuke declared curtly. "No doubt about it."

After a moment's hesitation, Tanjiro nodded. "Makes sense."

"So mean!" Zenitsu cried, practically shedding tears of blood. "Both of you are being way too mean! And like, what?! You're saying I'm not hot? That no girl could ever fall for me? I mean, Inosuke's one thing, but even *you* think that, Tanjiro? Acting like you're the good one?! Arrrrrrgh!"

"No. I mean, that's not what we're—" It was hard to finish that sentence. Unable to actually tell a lie, Tanjiro interrupted himself, flustered. "Anyway," he continued cheerfully, "let's hurry back to the Butterfly Mansion."

Shinobu was there at least. If Shinobu gently coaxed him with something like "A fortune? Don't let it get to you. Don't worry about a thing like that," Zenitsu would relax. And before long, the day would be over. Once tomorrow came, he'd forget all about the whole incident.

"Absolutely not!" Zenitsu said, as if something had snapped inside of him. "Not the Butterfly Mansion! Tanjiro!"

"Why not?" Tanjiro was baffled. He never dreamed Zenitsu would object to this. "What's wrong with the Butterfly Mansion?"

"You—! You really don't get it?! There are six girls in that house! You hear me? *Six!* Shinobu, Kanao, Aoi, Kiyo, Sumi, and Naho!" Zenitsu counted them off on his fingers.

Tanjiro still didn't know what Zenitsu was talking about. Inosuke also stared at Zenitsu with a look that said, "What is *with* this guy?"

"What does that matter, Zenitsu?" he finally asked.

"What happens if love blooms in one of their hearts?" Zenitsu spelled it out for him. "What if one of them comes to me with her arms open? I'll die, won't I? And it'll be so awful for her too! I mean, I'll have died because of her love, okay? It's just too terribly tragic!"

Tanjiro still didn't get it.

"Same old creepy little jerk." Inosuke muttered next to him.

Tanjiro was at a loss for what to say to his poor friend.

"I've decided," Zenitsu said, sounding strange, "I'm going to avoid, avoid, absolutely *avoid* girls all day today! Tanjiro, Inosuke! You have to protect me so that no girls fall in love with me! Okay? You'll protect me with everything you've got, right?! I have to stay alive for Nezuko's sake too!"

"Let's just leave him here," Inosuke said.

"No." Tanjiro sighed. "We can't do that."

Their words didn't reach Zenitsu. He was undoubtedly

thinking about something to do with Nezuko. He shed hot tears at whatever poignant scene he was imagining.

Watching from the side, it was pretty creepy.

"Okay, we go dump him somewhere."

"I told you, we can't go doing that, Inosuke."

"It's all right, Nezuko! I won't die on you! I just know I'll live through this crisis and make you the happiest girl alive! Don't worry. Marry me!"

Zenitsu clenched one hand tightly, utterly absorbed in his own delusion, and ignored Inosuke's biting words and Tanjiro's troubled face.

"Good afternoon!" a woman called out with a cheerful smile when they entered the building.

"Oh!"

Tanjiro had led his friends into a cafe along the road to appease both Zenitsu, who refused to go back to the Butterfly Mansion, and Inosuke, who had declared his hunger. But as soon as they were inside, Tanjiro knew he had made a huge mistake.

Why are there only women in here?

Because this was a stylish cafe in a big town, its seats were mostly filled with girls. All of these beautiful young ladies, decked out in their finest, were looking at the Demon Slayers. The smiling server wore a Western-style white apron over her kimono. With smooth black hair tied neatly, she turned gentle eyes on them.

"How many in your party?" she asked, and as feared, Zenitsu clutched Tanjiro's arm with one hand while he held the worn paper charm from the old woman tightly in his other hand, and began to tremble.

"Eeeeeeeee!" he squealed in a threatening manner.

"Eep!" The woman's smile froze.

"Please excuse him." Tanjiro stepped up to bow and apologize.

"R-right this way, then," she said, her voice suddenly an octave higher, and led them to a table in the back. She was so frightened that she didn't even notice Inosuke's boar head.

To Zenitsu in his current condition, however, her terrified mien appeared as that of a young maiden excited and bashful before him.

"What am I going to do oh no what am I going to do what am I going to do what am I going to do?" he muttered. "What if she falls for me…? What if she falls for me…? What if…?"

"Zenitsu," Tanjiro said.

"Haah hah! Haah! Hah! Hah! Haah fwoo! Hah!"

The heavy breathing, the excessive sweating, the constant shaking—it was all over the top, and Tanjiro could feel the tension radiating off Zenitsu's body. The panting and the sweat on his palms were particularly incredible.

"Hey, Zenitsu. Can you calm down just a little bit?" Tanjiro aired his complaint in a gentle tone, but Zenitsu's hackles still went up.

"Don't tell me what to do!" he snapped. "You're fine with me dying? Doesn't matter to you if I'm gone from this world? What kind of a friend are you?"

"That's not what I meant. Of course I'm not fine with you dying, Zenitsu. It's just, you don't need to be so afraid," he said, reassuringly, but his words failed to reach Zenitsu.

"What am I going to do what am I going to do?" He trembled and shook.

Troubled, Tanjiro glanced at Inosuke, who snorted in an "I told you so" kind of way. "I knew it," he said. "We shoulda tossed him somewhere."

"Don't say that," Tanjiro replied. "You're supposed to be the boss here, right, Inosuke?"

"Wellll. C'mon, Monitsu, here we go!" Suddenly in good

spirits, Inosuke whapped Zenitsu on the back. "I'll keep you safe. I'm the boss, after all."

The table the server led them to was in the very back of the cafe, in a corner far from the other tables. The space was otherwise bright, but for some reason this spot alone was dimly lit, the air stagnant.

The server clearly pushed them all the way to the hinterlands to keep them far from the other customers. This was actually a blessing at the moment, and Tanjiro was thankful.

Zenitsu took the inside seat and clutched his knees to his chest. Tanjiro sat next to him, and Inosuke across from him.

Menu in hand, the first thing Inosuke said was "I can't read it."

"This is 'a' in hiragana. This one's 'i.'" Tanjiro read the characters out one by one, like he used to for his little brothers. "The same 'i' as in your name, Inosuke."

"Lord Inosuke's 'i'!"

"This is 'su,' here's 'ku.'"

"Eeeeeeeeeeeee!!" Zenitsu shrieked from the chair beside him.

"What's wrong?" Tanjiro asked, stunned.

With a trembling hand, Zenitsu pointed at a girl sitting at a table across the room. "That girl looked at me and froze. She's fallen in love."

"Sorry. I don't understand at all what you're trying to say," Tanjiro said sadly.

Despair in his voice, Zenitsu shook his head in an exaggerated manner and said, "I mean, they're all looking at me. All the girls in this cafe have maybe fallen for me. Unnnh… What am I going to do, Tanjiro?"

"This guy's hopeless," Inosuke interjected.

"Inosuke," Tanjiro said in gentle rebuke.

"He was always a creep, but we're talking danger zone here. He can't tell the difference between fantasy and reality anymore."

"Inosuke," Tanjiro said again. His friend always came straight out with things, even when he shouldn't.

Another woman came then to take their order.

"Er… Have you decided?" Her voice was tense and trembled slightly, perhaps because she was clearly on guard against Zenitsu.

Getting the wrong idea once again, Zenitsu began to shake. "Eee! This woman keeps glancing at me. I just know she's going to ask me out… Scary scary scary scary so scared so scared so scared so scared—"

"Behave yourself." Tanjiro knocked Zenitsu on the head just as the yellow-haired boy was on the verge of exploding again. "She's just freaked out. Don't make trouble for the server!"

He didn't think he'd hit him that hard, but Zenitsu's eyes rolled back in his head, and he fell face-first onto the table like the thread of tension holding him up had been cut.

With Zenitsu finally quiet, Tanjiro bowed his head once more. "I'm sorry for all the fuss."

"I-it's fine." The woman had tears in her eyes.

Tanjiro wanted to release her as quickly as he could, but he didn't know what anything was by looking at the words on the menu.

Just when he was wondering what to do, Inosuke pointed and said, "Hey, doesn't that thing look good?"

Tanjiro looked over and saw a girl at a nearby table eating something that looked like a white manju in a glass dish, using a spoon. From the way the girl was eating, it seemed to be extremely cold, and something long and thin like a *senbei* cracker accompanied it. Tanjiro was curious what it tasted like.

"Three of those, please," he ordered.

"Right away." The woman smiled, obviously relieved, and hurried from their table.

"Here we are. Our specialty, *ais kreem*."

Their order was brought surprisingly fast, but it was yet another woman who carried it. This one looked fearsomely tough, with a physique that would make a sumo wrestler proud. Just one of her arms was more muscular than Tanjiro or Zenitsu's thighs, or even Inosuke himself.

"It melts quickly, so please enjoy it right away."

"Ooh! Thank you!" Tanjiro thanked her with a smile and noticed with trepidation that the woman's proud physique had roused the fighting instincts of the belligerent Inosuke. Tanjiro's heart was in his throat, worried that his friend would challenge her to a fight.

"Yahoo! I was sick of waiting!"

Fortunately, however, the feast in front of Inosuke's eyes entranced him, and he had no time for fighting. Tossing his boar head aside, Inosuke excitedly grabbed his spoon and brought a heaping spoonful of the white stuff to his mouth.

"O...oh," he moaned.

When Tanjiro looked at him, he was trembling with emotion.

"This is super amazing! What *is* this?!"

"She said it's called 'ais kreem.'" Tanjiro told him the name he'd heard from the server. And then he took a bite himself. "So good!"

His eyes grew round in surprise. It tasted totally different from a manju. Whatever this "ais kreem" was, it was surprisingly sweet and cold. But in his mouth, it melted and disappeared almost immediately.

"Yum yum yum, yum yum yum," Inosuke said loudly, scarfing the treat down. Inosuke was essentially harmless when he was eating delicious food. Plus, beneath that boar head, his face was unimaginably handsome, and he was quite the attractive, fair-skinned young man. Maybe that was why the eyes of the girls in the cafe were focused on him.

For some reason, that was the moment Zenitsu chose to wake up.

"Ah?!"

"Oh, you're awake, Zenitsu?" Tanjiro sighed with relief. "Your ais kreem's here. It's really good. I'm sure eating it will take your mind off things."

His words didn't reach his friend's ears. Zenitsu was as pale as a sheet of paper.

"I feel eyes on me…"

"Huh?" Tanjiro glanced at him.

"Not 'huh'!" Zenitsu cried. "Can't you feel how passionately these girls are looking at me? What am I going

to do? I'll die, you know! I'll die in the most gruesome way anyone could think up, okay?"

"Calm down, Zenitsu," he said soothingly. "You're bothering people."

"Nooo! Nezuko, Gramps, save meee! I don't want to dieee!"

"Zenitsu!" Tanjiro snapped at him.

"Excuse me, sir, but I'll have to ask you to step outside if you continue to make such a commotion," the tough woman warned softly.

Zenitsu stared at her. "Huh? What? Did you just say, 'Sir, I love you. I'm shy, so would you mind stepping outside'…?"

Mishearing her in an impossible way, he immediately began to shake. "Eeeeeeee! A confession of love! She's going to ask me out, this is how it starts! Nooooooooooooo!"

Shrieking at the top of his lungs, Zenitsu pushed Tanjiro out of the way and fled the cafe before Tanjiro even had the chance to call out and stop him.

"Zenitsu…" He stared after his friend, dumbfounded.

Maybe because Zenitsu was that upset, he had forgotten the paper charm he'd gripped so tightly.

Across from Tanjiro, Inosuke was absorbed in his "ais kreem" and hadn't noticed Zenitsu's departure. Tanjiro gently picked up the charm Zenitsu had left behind.

"Sir, that charm... Where did you get it?" the woman asked in a stern voice, frowning.

"Now what? Where did you go, Zenitsu?"

Tanjiro looked for his friend on the busy streets. If they were on the mountain, his yellow hair would have been easy to spot, but the town was filled with all kinds of color. People were dressed in an array of outfits, so finding Zenitsu would be a bit of work.

According to the server at the cafe—her name was Saya—there was a fake fortune-teller who passed herself off as the real famed fortune-teller of the crossroads. She had her fun scaring passersby with evil pronouncements. Saya said she'd had another customer come across this fake, and the charm they'd shown her was exactly the same as the one that Zenitsu had received. When Tanjiro told her about what had happened, Saya was deeply sympathetic.

"I'm off work in a bit here, so I'll help you look for him," said the kindhearted girl. "I know this town pretty well."

Tanjiro was delighted to have an extra pair of eyes on the job, but they still couldn't seem to find Zenitsu. *Zenitsu couldn't have fallen into despair and… No, he wouldn't do that.* Tanjiro was clearly flailing. All these terrible images kept popping up in his mind.

"Can't you *smell* that dodo?" Inosuke asked.

"I've been trying for a while, but there are so many other strong smells getting in the way. I can't pick out his scent." Tanjiro frowned.

Something Saya had told him was "perfume"—some kind of smelly water, apparently—wafted up from most of the women. This sea of scent confounded his nose, and his abnormally keen sense of smell was of no use.

"I'll check this area with Saya. Inosuke, you go—" Tanjiro began.

"Over there!" Saya shouted.

Tanjiro looked in the direction she was pointing and found that Zenitsu was indeed walking along the road there, crying. What a relief.

"Zen—" Tanjiro started to call out, but Saya yelled and interrupted him.

"Siiiiir!" She raced toward him.

Zenitsu shrieked and then collapsed on the ground.

His legs had surely given out in terror. He closed his eyes as if resigned to his fate.

"The carriage horse's run off!" A man's roar cut through the area.

At once, there was a huge commotion.

"Ruuuuuun!"

"Aaaaaaah!"

"Nooooo!"

People ran in circles, and screams filled the air.

Tanjiro looked around. He could see the horse to the right of Saya as she ran toward Zenitsu. The horse reared, raising its front legs high into the air.

"Inosuke!"

"Yup!"

At Tanjiro's word, the two Demon Slayers jumped into action at the same time.

Before they could reach the server, something like a bolt of lightning swept her out from under the horse's hooves.

"Hmm?" Tanjiro's eyes flew open in surprise.

That bolt of lightning was Zenitsu. He realized his fellow corps member had used Thunder Breathing to save Saya.

"Not half bad." He heard Inosuke murmur. "Nice work for a coward." Inosuke glared at the rampaging horse that had lost its target.

Instantly, the horse became as docile and submissive as a puppy.

That's Inosuke for you...

A relieved Tanjiro turned back to Zenitsu, who was holding Saya in the middle of an excited crowd.

"Way to go, boy!"

"What just happened? You were super fast!"

"You're so cool!"

"Amazing, young man!"

They heaped praise on Zenitsu one after the other, but the boy in question looked like compliments were the last thing he cared about. His face was pale, and while Saya may have been heavy in his arms, he was trembling too much for that to be the only reason.

"Zenitsu, are you okay?"

Tanjiro tried to run over, but the crowd was in the way, preventing him from getting close. He managed to push his way to the front just in time to see Saya look up at Zenitsu with a strangely bewitched expression.

"Sir, you did that for *me*?"

"N-no no no." Zenitsu shook his head quickly back and forth. "I-i-i-i-i-it was nothing special. A-a-as a human being, I only did w-w-w-what was natural."

"Such a humble and gallant man," Saya murmured, enraptured. The mood felt very much like she would confess her newfound love for him at any second.

Zenitsu desperately looked anywhere but at the girl in his arms. His gaze roamed the crowd of onlookers, pleadingly, and then froze in place. His face grew even paler, like that of a corpse.

Tanjiro followed Zenitsu's gaze and saw the fake fortune-teller who had started all of this.

"Inosuke!" he cried.

"I got her!" Inosuke leaped toward the old woman, parting the crowd as he went.

However…

"Huh? S-sir?" Saya cried. "Are you all right?! Sirrr?!"

Tanjiro hurriedly turned back toward Zenitsu. His friend had fainted, still holding Saya in his arms.

He later explained everything to Zenitsu and placated Inosuke, who wanted to pluck out all of the fake fortune-teller's hair after catching her. They then left the town

behind them with Saya waving goodbye. The trio reached the Butterfly Mansion just as the sun set completely.

"My goodness, you've had quite a rough time, hm?" Shinobu said sympathetically after hearing their story.

Kiyo, Sumi, and Naho also expressed their indignation— "Poor Zenitsu!" and "Are you all right?" and "Lying like that, how awful!" Zenitsu, who had truly felt down in the dumps, cheered right up.

It turned out that Saya was the cafe owner's beloved niece, and as thanks for saving her, the owner had sent them on their way with their arms piled with chocolates, caramels, and other sweets. The girls at the mansion were delighted, of course.

And their happiness was Zenitsu's happiness.

"Inosuke kept his cool right from the start, though," Tanjiro remarked, as he sipped the tea Aoi and Kanao had made for them.

"Huh?" Inosuke lifted his face from the treat he was eating. Chocolate was smeared all over his cheeks.

"What a mess!" Aoi scolded him.

"It's because he doesn't think girls could like me," Zenitsu sulked. "Or else he didn't care what happened to me, so he was super calm. This jerk."

Surprisingly, Inosuke said something to the contrary. "It's 'cause that old hag gave me a bad feeling the second we met her. It was like she'd already decided what she was going to say and she was licking her chops, looking for who to say it to. A real fortune-teller wouldn't do that, right? And like, what about those sounds you're always hearing? You didn't hear it?"

Zenitsu's eyebrows jumped up, and his jaw dropped ever so slightly. It was a face that said he'd completely forgotten about this particular skill of his. He dropped his head and fell silent.

"You really are a dodo." Inosuke struck the killing blow. "How about changing your name to Dodoitsu?"

"Shut up," Zenitsu said. But there was none of the usual force in his voice.

Tanjiro was in the same place. Kanao poured fresh tea into his empty cup, and he reflected on how much the fake fortune-teller's words had shaken him and how he hadn't been able to smell the malice that spilled out from her.

"Thanks."

Kanao wordlessly glanced at him.

"Did you have some chocolate, Kanao? It's really good." He offered her some, but Kanao turned red for some reason and ducked behind the nearby Aoi. She hadn't tossed a coin, so she couldn't accept it? No, it didn't seem like that was it.

What's wrong, I wonder? Tanjiro cocked his head slightly to one side.

"Hold on just a minute there," Zenitsu said suddenly. "It's getting *awfully* cozy over there. Huh, Tanjiro?"

"What?" Tanjiro frowned. "Why do you have that scary look on your face?"

"Walking around looking all innocent! If you find happiness before me, I'll curse you, you know?" Jealousy at full throttle, Zenitsu pushed his way toward Tanjiro, gritting his teeth. He seemed ready to lay that curse on Tanjiro that very second, if not sooner.

"Huh?"

Tanjiro was flustered. He had absolutely no idea what Zenitsu was talking about.

"Now, now," Shinobu said calmly. "Everything turned out all right, Zenitsu. Plus, you three caught a fake fortune-teller on your way home from a mission. You must really be good friends, hm?"

She pulled everyone in the room together with a smile.

Aoi heated some water for them, so the three Demon Slayers headed for the bath.

"I don't want to take a bath," Inosuke complained. "Cold shower's fine."

Tanjiro dragged him along anyway, and then from behind, he heard a small voice.

"Thanks for helping me, Tanjiro. Inosuke." The voice really was very quiet, curiously earnest, almost embarrassed.

"Zenitsu?" When Tanjiro looked over his shoulder, Zenitsu was already his usual self again.

"Aaah, what a miserable day," he muttered, looking entirely fed up. "I'm getting in first." He trotted for the bath.

Tanjiro quietly smiled as his stubborn friend walked away.

"You must really be good friends, hm?"

Shinobu's words came back to him. Were they good friends? He wasn't too sure, maybe because they'd been by his side ever since he became a corps member. Yet, he was happy that it had been these two he met on the mission at the drum house. They'd been able to overcome certain things simply because they were together. He'd been able to keep going without unendurable sadness overwhelming him. It was a happy thing not to be alone.

CHAPTER 3 CHRONICLE OF A FORTUNE-TELLING FUSS

"I'll get in, but I'm not washing."

"No way. Aoi told you, didn't she? You have to wash properly before you get in the tub."

"That noisy little runt!"

"You can't go saying things like that. They do all this for us. Come on. Let's go, Inosuke." Yanking his boar-head friend behind him, Tanjiro smiled again.

Outside the veranda, the stars in the night sky glittered and twinkled, as if any one of them could turn into a shooting star at any moment.

Chapter 4
AOI AND KANAO

I'm just not very good with Kanao.

Still, it's not that I hate her. She's never done anything to me, and we've never actually butted heads or anything. It's just that she's hard to be around.

If I had to say, Kanao Tsuyuri is like a doll. She doesn't answer when you say something to her. She's constantly wearing that empty smile, and she can't make a decision on her own—she always has to toss a coin.

I'm short-tempered, so I get cross with her. Sometimes, I just want to throw my hands up and be done with her.

Agewise, I'm the older one, but in terms of rank, Kanao's much higher than me. She's so full of Demon Slayer talent that, even though she's still young, she was chosen as a Tsuguko, an apprentice to the Hashira.

On the other hand, I survived the Final Selection on nothing more than luck. I'm a coward, and I'll never make my name in actual battle because I'm terrified of fighting demons. Thanks to Lady Shinobu's merciful ways, I can stay here at the Butterfly Mansion, take care of injured corps members, and help them with their recovery training.

Does a Demon Slayer who can't kill demons have any value? Of course not. I'm a burden on the corps. Maybe that's why I get strangely out of sorts with Kanao. Once I realized

it was more or less an inferiority complex, my own pettiness annoyed me. I was hating myself more and more.

And then he came along and said to me, "You helped me, Aoi. So you're now a part of me. I'll think about you when I go into battle."

He said that someone as useless as me was a part of him, that he would take all these feelings with no outlet into battle with him… He said it without affectation or hesitation, with a smile like the sun.

So I decided to try. I decided to throw myself into whatever I actually could do. *And yet…*

When the Sound Hashira ordered me to accompany him on a mission, I started shaking all over. I remembered the terror of confronting a demon. I couldn't even keep him from snatching up Naho.

"Kanao! Kanao!!" I kept shouting, like a fool.

And Kanao grabbed my hand. Without tossing a coin, her brow furrowed and teeth gritted, she held my hand tightly, ignoring the Sound Hashira as he yelled at her.

I still haven't been able to thank her for that.

"Shopping?"

"Yes. I'd love it if the two of you would go."

Her superior, Shinobu, had called her to her room, so Aoi had assumed she would be taken to task for the Sound Hashira incident. But that wasn't what happened.

It felt strange to be told to go shopping together. Aoi stole a glance at Kanao sitting next to her. She was staring into space with the same expression as always on her face. Aoi had no idea what was going on in her head.

"I wrote down here the medicines that I want you to buy," Shinobu said, and smiled.

If the old her had been asked to run errands with the silent Kanao, it would have been a hard request to accept, even if it was Shinobu doing the asking—as much as she loved and respected her.

But for Aoi at the moment, it was a welcome lifeline. She bowed her head, thinking she'd finally be able to thank Kanao. "I understand. We'll go, then."

"Thank you very much. We'll need all these because Tanjiro and the others will most likely return here when their current mission is over," Shinobu continued lightly.

This startled Aoi.

"Now, Uzui's with them, so there's probably no need to be concerned. But let's be as prepared as possible while we wait for them."

Aoi accepted the instructions silently. They had gone on that mission in Aoi's place. *Because I'm pathetic.* She gently bit her lip. She sincerely hoped that it wasn't a dangerous mission. But this was a self-serving wish. If a Hashira was on the job, then it couldn't have been simply to round up some small-fry demon.

When they went to dispatch the demon lurking in the Infinity Train, they came back battered and bruised all over. The mission inflicted wounds on both body and mind, and they were so black-and-blue that it was painful just to look at them.

This time, all of those injuries would be because of her. *Please, please be safe*, she prayed, practically in tears. *You all have to make it back here together.*

The tips of her fingers on her lap trembled. She willed them to be still, but the shaking didn't stop. Aoi closed her eyes firmly at her own cowardliness.

The wholesale chemist where Shinobu was a regular stood in a town a little way from the Butterfly Mansion. Aoi had been there any number of times, trailing along behind Shinobu.

"Welcome."

She recognized the manager who greeted them. He was too thin and had a face like a shriveled eggplant.

"Hello, we were hoping to buy some medicines," Aoi replied.

Since Kanao didn't speak as a general rule, Aoi held Shinobu's list in one hand and asked for the items they needed. She wasn't particularly anxious about her ability to pick out medicine, at least.

But when it came time to pay, the color drained from her face. She was sure she'd brought her wallet, and yet it wasn't there. The wallet into which she'd carefully tucked the money from Shinobu was nowhere to be found. She desperately fumbled around in the pockets of her corps uniform, and then put a hand to her mouth.

Ah…

She suddenly remembered that she'd pulled it out of her uniform to pay someone just as they were leaving the mansion and that she'd left it on the table there.

Astonishing. It was an unthinkable error. She froze
in shock.

Kanao peered at her, as if sensing something.

"Kanao, I'm sorry," Aoi said in a hoarse voice, bowing so
deeply her nose practically touched her kneecaps. "I forgot
my wallet!"

There was no response from Kanao.

She was so ashamed and miserable, she wanted to
disappear even more than before.

In a turn of bad luck, neither she nor Kanao had brought
along their personal wallets since they were only going out to
do the shopping.

Kanao stared hard at her coin and began to blanch.

Aoi smiled lifelessly and said, "I would never take that
away from you."

They had been to this shop countless times, and so she
pushed aside her embarrassment and asked to start a tab.
The deeply wary manager simply would not agree to it.

"Ask all you want, but this is a business. Unfortunately, the owner's out today, and I don't have the authority," he said, before muddying the conversation with a question. "And what exactly is it that you all do? This 'corps' of yours, what sort of group is it really?"

"What?" Aoi was at a loss for words. At times like this, not belonging to an official government organization made things difficult.

Because no one believed them when they talked about demons and all the rest, the social trust toward the Demon Slayer Corps was definitely not high, except among the Wisteria Houses. The Demon Slayers risked their lives and fought demons for people, but they weren't even granted permission to wear their Nichirin swords.

When Aoi was stuck for a reply, the manager looked at the two girls with hard eyes.

"What do you do with nothing but women out there? The one who came last time was strangely provocative. You're not actually involved in some shameful business, now, are you?"

"I—!"

This sort of baseless rumor spread because it was only ever women who came from the Butterfly Mansion to do the

shopping. Aoi was furious at how coarsely the manager was looking at them.

"I understand. No need for a tab! Good day!" she announced politely. She left the shop, dragging Kanao behind her—and instantly regretted the act.

Now I've done it...

She held her head in her hands. There was no way they would make it back to town while the shop was still open if they returned to the Butterfly Mansion now to get her wallet. She really should have controlled her temper. She should have kept bowing her head and stayed quiet, no matter what the man said to her. She simply couldn't hold her tongue when it came to Shinobu or the corps being disrespected.

I'm an idiot. Stupid stupid stupid!

Just when she'd decided to move forward so as not to waste the kindness of the words that boy had spoken to her that day. Her feelings always raced ahead of her. It was pathetic how she was always running in circles.

All of the things they were supposed to buy that day—the medicines, the sake for medical purposes, the cotton for bandages—they were all essential and indispensable. What if the Demon Slayers returned and the mansion wasn't all stocked up? What if they were so seriously injured that even

Shinobu couldn't handle it? *What if the worst happens to them because of me?*

Just picturing it, she felt her legs tremble wretchedly. Her own idiocy made her field of view go dark.

"I'm sorry, Kanao." This trip was turning out not to be the right place to express her gratitude to the younger girl.

Hanging her head dejectedly, Aoi turned toward Kanao and bowed once more. "I was already plenty deadweight before, being too scared of demons to go on a mission. To think I can't even do the shopping right… I really am the worst."

As she spoke, tears threatened to spill out of her eyes. She desperately held them back. The base of her throat grew hot, and she felt a pang inside of her nose. "I… Even *I* know I'm pathetic."

Kanao watched her in response, saying nothing.

"I'll try asking again. I'll see if I can bring the money tomorrow." She was about to turn away when Kanao's hand reached out to her. Kanao patted Aoi's head awkwardly.

This was not a typically feminine soft hand. This was the hand of a girl who had trained and worked until the skin grew thick. This hand had fought to protect someone, and at its touch, Aoi's tears stopped.

"Kanao?" she said, confused.

The girl smiled the tiniest bit and took Aoi's hand. With-out an "are you okay?" or a "let's go," she started walking.

"Are we going back to the Butterfly Mansion?" Aoi asked the girl silently pulling on her hand.

Kanao didn't say anything. Not "yes," not "no."

"But this isn't the way back to the… And we still need the medicine." Aoi hesitated, looking back over her shoulder at the shop steadily growing distant behind them.

But Kanao kept on walking, as though she hadn't heard Aoi.

Aoi sighed and resigned herself to the situation. It was things like this that made her not understand Kanao.

After walking for a bit, Kanao abruptly stopped. The road was packed with people.

"What's this?"

Aoi took a hard look. It seemed that they were doing some-thing in front of the local drinking establishment.

Maybe some kind of show? she wondered absently.

"Oh dear! What adorable girls you are," said an elegantly dressed older woman standing nearby. "Go on ahead and watch." She half dragged them forward.

"Oh no, we're—"

"Now that I'm looking at you, I feel like I've seen you somewhere, haven't I? Don't be shy. Have a peek. They're neck and neck on the sweets."

Aoi ended up peering at the tavern through the gaps between the other spectators and saw that a number of men and women were competing in an eating contest. Now that she thought about it, eating and drinking contests had been everywhere in the Edo era, but they had essentially dropped off the map as popular entertainment these days.

Forty-five manju, seven large bars of *yokan* jelly, seventy *uguisumochi* mini-cakes, four *takuan* daikon radishes. Voices cried out unbelievable numbers, and Aoi doubted her ears.

The appetite of the sumo wrestler taking up center stage was especially remarkable. He polished off a yokan bar in a split second and then stuffed manju after manju into his mouth. Just watching him was nearly enough to give her heartburn, but Aoi was more curious about Kanao's reaction.

She hadn't heard it directly from Kanao herself, but apparently her parents had been so poor that they had sold her to a procurer. Shinobu and her late sister rescued her from that fate and brought her up as a Demon Slayer.

Aoi was worried about what she would think of all this.

"Kanao?"

She glanced at Kanao timidly and found that the girl was staring blankly at the spectacle with the same emotionless expression with which she looked at everything else. A massive amount of food was being consumed—not because the people eating were hungry, not for the purpose of staying alive, but for sheer entertainment. Looking at the girl's face in profile, Aoi felt like she could hardly stand it for some reason.

"Let's go." This time, Aoi took Kanao's hand. She gripped it tightly, and Kanao looked up at Aoi curiously, without a word. They were about to leave when several people screamed.

"Wh—?!"

Aoi looked back and found that the sumo wrestler had collapsed. A half-eaten manju dropped from his hand and rolled away.

"Unh! Unh... Unh... Unh!"

The young wrestler's face was ashen as he groaned for a moment or two. His eyes rolled back in his head before long, and he lost consciousness. He was frothing at the mouth. The spectators screamed once more.

"W-what?"

"Did he get some manju stuck in his throat?"

"Hey! Pry his mouth open!"

"Should we give him some water?"

Aoi heard some men in the crowd talking. It sounded like they were going to take some misguided measures in an effort to help the wrestler.

They can't.

The moment she had the thought, her body was already moving.

"Excuse me! Excuse me. Please let me through! Let me through!"

She forced her way to the center of the crowd and knelt down beside the sumo wrestler. She checked his breathing, his pulse, his pupils, the inside of his mouth, and the sound coming from his stomach, in that order. The color drained from her face.

I knew it. This is more serious than him simply having something stuck in his throat.

To be blunt, his condition was rather serious. Shinobu would have been able to help him if she had been there, but the only one there now was Aoi.

Could she do it? Take someone else's life into her hands? After all, she couldn't even face a demon. *But if I don't, he'll...*

Aoi bit her lip hard and recalled the emergency procedures

written in the medical books she'd read. She took a deep breath and called out to the spectators surrounding them, "This man could die unless we take action right now! Please, someone hurry and get a doctor!"

"G-got it! I'll go!" a man shouted and ran off.

Then Aoi looked at Kanao beside her. "Kanao, go talk to the owner of the tavern and get the following items."

Impatiently, she listed the bare minimum of things she would need to treat the wrestler. And then she remembered that that wasn't enough to set Kanao in motion.

"Your coin—"

She looked over her shoulder and saw Kanao's back as the girl raced inside the building. She paused.

It hadn't been an order from Shinobu, their superior, and Kanao hadn't tossed a coin to decide. She'd listened to Aoi and was doing as she asked. Confused and moved, Aoi turned back to her patient.

"Hey, you!" came a voice from the crowd, and a man with his hands stuffed in his pockets stepped forward. It was clear at first glance that he was no upstanding member of society.

"What's going on, little lady? I bet a fair chunk of money on this sumo wrestler. If he's got something stuck in his throat, get him to chuck it up, and then he can keep going. Don't go making out like it's some huge deal and getting in the way of my win. Got it?"

His breath reeked of alcohol. In all likelihood, he'd been placing bets with his friends. Unhappy at the abrupt interruption to the contest, he reached out toward the wrestler. Aoi stiffened and slapped his hand away.

"Did you not hear me?" she said. "This man's life is in danger. He needs immediate treatment."

"Hnh?" He arched an eyebrow at her.

"You're in the way. Please get back."

"What the—you little—" The look on his face changed, and he tried to grab her.

Aoi deftly dodged, caught hold of the man's arm, and flipped him onto his back. Even if she was a failure as a corps member, she had still made it through that training hell. A man like this was nothing to her.

"I believe I said to get back."

"Y-you…!"

"If you will not kindly cooperate, next time I will break your arm," she announced coolly, narrowing her eyes. The man gulped loudly.

Perhaps her threat worked. The man left, albeit cursing the whole while and spitting out the standard "I'll get you for this!" before vanishing.

To the suddenly excited crowd, Aoi said, "Everyone, please be quiet."

Having driven her point home, Aoi shifted the wrestler's body. When she had secured his airway, she saw Kanao racing toward her with all the things she needed.

"If this girl hadn't been here, this sumo wrestler might well have died," said the doctor who came running over at last. The remaining spectators let out a cheer.

"You did it!"

"Nice work!"

Aoi could hear people shouting here and there in the crowd.

"Aah, you girls are really something." The old woman who had urged them to the front earlier was one of those people.

She looked at them admiringly and then slapped the plump shoulder of the tavern master and sponsor of the contest.

"Come now, Yoshitaro. You make sure you thank these girls properly. If you'd had someone die on you, you'd be in a real tight spot right about now, hm? Give them a generous reward." Her attitude was friendly, and it was clear that the two of them knew each other.

"I will, fine. Honestly, I'm no match for you, Okayo." The master turned to Aoi and Kanao. "Thank you so much for your help. Please, take these with you as a small token of our gratitude."

Aoi was taken aback when he held out a cask of sake and a barrel of rice. She found she couldn't respond.

Intended for the victor of the contest, neither was what could be called a "small token," nor were they so easily carried with them. Nevertheless, Aoi was glad for the sake, which they had been planning to buy anyway, and they could make some money selling the rice. When she thought about how they'd be able to buy the medication and bandages, the weight of the barrels no longer seemed like a serious issue.

They split their reward between them, and Kanao started out ahead of Aoi once more. Her stride was easy and calm,

while Aoi staggered along behind her. Kanao was again leading her in the opposite direction from the road home to the Butterfly Mansion.

As Aoi wondered what was going on in her head, she suddenly remembered, *Oh, right. Thanks. I have to tell Kanao thank you.* She had to thank Kanao for the whole incident with the Sound Hashira, and also for what she had done back there. Kanao had listened to Aoi and responded promptly, enabling them to save that sumo wrestler. It would have been difficult for Aoi to have managed all on her own.

"Uh. Um. Hey, Kanao?" she called out to the back bearing the rice ahead of her.

Kanao stopped and looked over her shoulder at Aoi.

"Um. I just."

Kanao stared at her, waiting for her to continue. *You have to say it*, she told herself. When she actually tried to form the words, she felt strangely awkward. As Aoi groped for the right thing to say, she heard a thunderous, angry roar.

"You cow! If you're gonna kill me, then kill me already!"

"Don't think I won't! I'll kill you, all right! You useless good-for-nothing!"

"What?!" Aoi froze in place.

She heard a spectacular crash as something shattered, followed by a child crying.

"W-what's that? What's going on?" Aoi whirled her head around.

Kanao silently pointed toward a house in a back alley behind a paperer's shop, no doubt Kanao's way of saying that was the source of the commotion.

Aoi stepped into the narrow alley to find a row house with a frontage of just under three meters. A so-called partitioned longhouse. One of the sliding doors was half-open, and broken bowls and cups were scattered on the ground outside.

Aoi swallowed hard. "Excuse me!" she called. "Are you all right?"

A tall, skinny man came flying—almost tumbling—out. A woman rushed out after him with a baby on her back. Aoi gasped when she saw what was in the woman's hand: she held a broad-bladed carving knife that shone dully. Aoi could hear children crying inside the gloomy house.

"Today my patience finally runs out," the woman snarled. "I'm going to carve him into pieces! This simpleton of a husband!"

"I'd like to see you try!" the husband shouted. "You fat cow!"

"What did you say?! Go ahead and say that one more time! I dare you!"

"Oh, I'll say it! I'll say it until the stars fall from the sky! You enormous pig!"

Furious at her husband's abuse, the woman yanked him up by his collar with a plump hand. The man shrieked like a stuck pig, which jolted Aoi out of her dumbfounded staring.

"Please stop this!" she cried. "He will really die, you know!"

"Don't try and stop me! This is none of your business!" The woman glared at her with bloodshot eyes.

Aoi didn't flinch at the ferocity of the woman's gaze. Instead, she pulled the couple apart and asked, "Why are you so angry?"

"This lout spent all our earnings on drink and gambling! The rice box is empty! We've got no savings! The whole family's going to starve to death now!" The woman went on and on, before pushing her husband away and dropping to her knees. She began to sob, and the cries that slipped out from those parched lips were almost like the howls of a wild beast.

"O-Omitsu." The husband looked anxiously at his wife. "S-sorry. Just hang in there. I mean, you know I'm sorry." He pressed his forehead to the ground in apology.

A boy came out of the tenement then, pulling a small girl by the hand. They were maybe seven and five. The girl was crying, and her older brother was desperately trying to hold back his own tears.

"Mom, don't cry," he consoled his mother earnestly. "I'll work real hard!"

The kind face of the strong-willed boy overlapped with that of a certain Demon Slayer in her mind.

"Don't cry! When I grow up, I'll work a lot and become really rich, and I'll make sure you have a great life!"

At the boy's admirable declaration, Aoi gave Kanao a quick signal with her eyes, but Kanao didn't notice. She was staring at the sobbing family with narrowed eyes. She looked as if she were seeing something very far away, something she could never have again.

"Kanao," Aoi said gently. "The rice."

Kanao finally picked up on Aoi's intent and nodded. She let the barrel of rice slide off of her back to the ground.

"Please take this," Aoi said, and the couple lifted their heads, surprised. "It should be enough to tide you over for a while. And you could also sell some for money."

"Really, miss—I mean, do you mean that, young lady?" the wife cried. "But we couldn't."

"Please promise me, though, that you won't use the money from selling this rice to buy sake or gamble," Aoi said.

"I-I won't! This is just so—" The man pledged, his hands together as if in prayer. "I'm a new man. I'm reborn. I'll never for the life of me do anything to hurt my wife and children again!"

"All right, then." Aoi turned on her heel. She was about to step out into the road when the wife called out to them.

"You'd do this for us when we're total strangers?"

Aoi hesitated. She didn't really know what to say. She'd just wanted to help the boy who was so desperate to help his parents. She'd wanted to help a mother who would choose to starve as a family rather than so much as consider selling one of her children, even in such poverty. That was all.

Aoi felt like it was a bit different from wanting to help. She felt like "I wanted to help" was an extremely arrogant way of putting it. In the end, she said nothing and left the alley.

"Miss ladies! Waaaaait!"

The boy chased after them, yanking his little sister along by the hand.

"Thank you… Thank you so much!" he said and bowed deeply. The little girl also dipped her head in imitation of her big brother. "My dad sells these, so."

The boy dug in his kimono and held out a pinwheel. He likely was giving it to them as a thank-you, but Aoi hesitated to accept it.

Considering his family's situation, it was hard to believe that this was *just* a pinwheel. They could sell it for cash.

But Kanao reached out and took the pinwheel from the boy. Without even flipping her coin. Even so, it was an extremely natural movement with no hesitation whatsoever.

"Thanks," Kanao said in a small voice, and the boy beamed. It was a bright smile from the bottom of his heart.

Aoi felt a sharp pang in her own heart as she watched him.

The boy pulled his sister along behind him, headed back to their family home, repeatedly thanking them as he went.

Aoi stared at Kanao, and Kanao blew on the pinwheel in her hand. The red wheel went round and round.

"Why?" Aoi asked.

Why were you able to accept that so easily?

Why didn't you flip your coin?

For a while, Kanao stared at the spinning pinwheel, but eventually she said slowly, "This was…that boy's—the feelings in his heart."

"Ah!"

"He would have been hurt if we didn't accept it."

Aoi stared at Kanao with wide eyes, speechless. There was a huge lump in her throat; she couldn't say anything.

At the same time, she was embarrassed by her own hopeless foolishness. She'd been thinking it was arrogant to want to "help them," but she had nonetheless hesitated to accept the boy's thanks. In her heart, she had sympathized with their impoverished condition. But if they hadn't accepted the boy's thanks, then their own actions would have been complete charity. And the boy did not want to be the sad recipient of handouts. Kanao had understood that, so she'd been able to easily accept the pinwheel.

And meanwhile, I...

She was an extraordinarily half-hearted hypocrite. Aoi hung her head in self-loathing, and Kanao turned to her as if to urge her to come along. Aoi trailed after her dejectedly.

This again wasn't the road back to the Butterfly Mansion, but she no longer cared. After she followed Kanao for a bit, a large red umbrella came into view. *A teahouse*, Aoi thought absently.

Kanao whirled her head around in front of the teahouse, as if looking for someone. She then asked an old man, who appeared to be the owner of the teahouse, something in a quiet voice.

"Kanroji?" the man replied. "Oh, you mean Mitsuri? She's not here today." Kanao looked crestfallen.

Mitsuri? Probably Mitsuri Kanroji, the Love Hashira. She and Shinobu were good friends. Now that Aoi was thinking about it, she'd heard that Mitsuri was a regular at a teahouse in this area. Apparently, the *sanshoku dango* dumplings were scrumptious.

Why would Kanao be looking for the Love Hashira? Maybe she has a message for her from Shinobu? In that case, wouldn't she have come straight over here after they left the chemist's? And if Kanao had a message to give, Aoi would have also been informed of the errand.

She suddenly put a hand to her mouth. *Oh…*

She could think of only one reason for them to be there.

"You weren't *actually* going to borrow money from the Love Hashira, were you?" she asked Kanao.

After a moment's hesitation, Kanao nodded. "Because you were in trouble, Aoi."

Aoi didn't know how to respond.

"I thought maybe. But I couldn't help at all."

Warm droplets of water ran down Aoi's cheeks as she stood there. The tears she'd worked so hard to hold back spilled out of her eyes.

Kanao seemed surprised as she watched this, and finally she reached out to place a tentative hand on Aoi's shoulder.

"Thanks," Aoi murmured in a hoarse voice. Suddenly, her heart felt lighter. "You've helped me out in so many ways today. And when the Sound Hashira was about to carry me away, you held my hand…and you didn't let go. Thank you."

Kanao looked troubled, turning her face downward as if embarrassed.

I finally told her, Aoi thought.

"If I was alone," Kanao said quietly, "I wouldn't have known what to do when that sumo wrestler collapsed or when that couple was fighting."

"Kanao…" Aoi's eyes grew damp once more. "When did you start making decisions without flipping your coin?"

Kanao was silent for a moment.

"Tanjiro." She voiced an unexpected name. "He told me. 'You have to live by your heart,' he said. 'You can do it'… So…"

Ohh. Is that *it?* Aoi understood everything when she saw Kanao's pale cheeks flush red. Just as Tanjiro's words had freed Aoi from guilt and a deep-rooted inferiority complex, they had also changed Kanao.

The boy like the sun had turned the girl like a doll into a person. That was why Kanao had such a gentle and peaceful look on her face now.

Aoi looked at her, and her heart swirled with emotion. A warmth that made her want to cry. A hint of sadness that the boy hadn't only offered his words to her. And a childlike joy, like she and Kanao were sharing something that was for the two of them and no one else.

All this time she'd lived with this girl but felt that she was somehow far away. Now she felt so very close. Kanao was there, right beside her. Aoi stared silently at the girl's flushed cheeks.

"Come now. Eat up," the elderly proprietor said, carrying out a tray laden with tea and sanshoku dango. He set it down on the edge of the bench next to them and started to walk away.

"Huh? No, we…"

When Aoi confessed that they didn't have any money, the elderly man gave them a bittersweet smile and said, "I wouldn't take any from you. You're Mitsuri's friends, aren't you? Demon Slayers?"

"Oh." Aoi nodded. "Yes. We are."

"My daughter, you know, when she was attacked by a demon, Mitsuri saved her. If I had to say, well, I could never repay that debt."

Aoi listened in silence as the man continued.

"It's a tough job, but you keep at it. Just don't go pushing yourselves, all right?" he offered and went back inside the teahouse.

Aoi contemplatively looked back and forth between the owner's bent back and the steam rising up from the teacups. The unadorned words of gratitude, the kind gaze, the faint warmth in her heart...

The old her would have said something servile like, "In that case, I cannot accept such a kindness. I'm a coward who can't even set foot onto the battlefield."

But she didn't feel like that anymore. As a member of the Demon Slayer Corps, finding someone who understood and appreciated the corps overwhelmed her with delight. Aoi made a tiny sniff.

"Should we gratefully accept this, Kanao?" she asked with a smile, and Kanao nodded firmly, a smile on her own face.

The sanshoku dango recommended by the Love Hashira were indeed delicious and just the slightest bit salty.

As they left the teahouse, the western sky glowed red. Aoi walked with Kanao through the twilight town. Long shadows stretched out at their feet.

When they got back to the Butterfly Mansion, she would apologize for not being able to buy the medicine and come back to get it first thing the next morning. With this thought in her mind, they started out on the road home.

Once they had reached the outskirts of town, she got the sense that someone was chasing them.

"Hey! You there! You girls! Wait!"

"Hm?"

Aoi looked back to find the shriveled eggplant face of the chemist.

"Haah haah! Aah, thank goodness," he said, panting.

After waiting for him to get his breathing back under control, Aoi asked, "What is it?"

The chemist smiled awkwardly. "I'm really sorry about this afternoon."

He handed them a neatly wrapped package with the medicines Aoi had tried to buy.

"You pay up whenever you can."

"What? But…"

Aoi furrowed her brow at the chemist's sudden change
of heart. Kanao also stared at him curiously. The chemist
shrugged awkwardly, probably because the girls were looking
at him dubiously, instead of happily, as they wondered what
wind had changed.

"The truth is, you see…" He lowered his voice, as if
concerned about being overheard.

"So the older woman you met at the eating contest was the
chemist's own mother?" Shinobu asked Aoi delightedly when
Aoi had finished giving her a rundown of the day's events.

"Yes," Aoi confirmed.

"My goodness," she said admiringly. "What a surprising
coincidence."

The chemist's mother, now retired, had apparently seen
Shinobu, Kanao, and Aoi at the shop countless times.
Although Western clothes were no longer particularly

unusual, the uniforms of the Demon Slayer Corps were distinctive and had made an impression on her, it seemed. She'd just remembered where she'd seen Aoi and Kanao before when she returned to the shop and heard about the events of that afternoon. She was furious.

"Do you have holes where your eyes should be?! Turning such lovely girls away emptyhanded? Business, you know, it isn't just about chasing profits, now is it? Didn't I beat that into your head?! Come on now, go find them! Damned fool of a son!"

The chemist apparently flew out of the shop with his mother's roars following closely after him.

"Not only that, but she spoke to the fabric store owner, who's a friend of hers, and we were able to buy what we needed there too and pay later," Aoi said.

"Well, well!" Shinobu laughed. "This mother of his is quite frightening, hm? Nicely done, Aoi."

Aoi shook her head so hard, it threatened to fly off. A cold sweat sprang up on her brow. "N-not at all! To begin with, it was my fault for forgetting my wallet. It just happened to work out because Kanao was there."

"Kanao said the same thing," Shinobu told her.

"What?"

"Did you manage to say to her what you wanted to tell her?"

"Wh—?!" Aoi lifted her face in surprise.

Shinobu's gaze softened. "From the look of you, I'd say you did manage it, then."

"Lady Shinobu…"

"Struggling with things is definitely not a waste of time. It's necessary to train the mind and become stronger," Shinobu said. "But I want you to at least remember this. You, Kanao, Kiyo, Sumi, Naho—you're all my valuable helpers, my precious family."

Without uttering another word at her superior's beautiful smile, Aoi set her hands down on the floor and deeply bowed her head. Perhaps Shinobu had noticed Aoi's complicated feelings toward Kanao and sent the two of them shopping together in the hope that something like this would result.

A complex mix of feelings welled up in her and filled her heart. For a time, Aoi was unable to raise her head.

When she left Shinobu's room, it was completely dark outside. The pale light of the moon poured in through the latticed window.

Aoi had to put away the medicines they'd bought, cut the cotton, make bandages… Right, while she was at it, she should

also set out some sleepwear and futons for the corps members so that they'd be ready when Zenitsu, Inosuke, Nezuko, and Tanjiro—the Demon Slayers who risked their lives to fight the demons—came back injured.

After all, I'm a member of the Demon Slayer Corps too. She tightened her hands into fists. She was surprised at herself. This was possibly the first time since she'd survived the Final Selection that she'd felt so happy and purposeful.

Would she someday be able to live with her head held high and not have the fact that she'd survived weigh on her conscience? Would she come to like herself just the way she was?

You're going to be all right, a voice said. Whose voice was it? It might have been Tanjiro's, or maybe Shinobu's, or perhaps Kanao's. Aoi's lips spread into a slight smile at how naturally Kanao's name had come out.

"Aoiiiii!" Naho called, sounding troubled. "One of the corps members on bed rest is asking about their bandages. What do you want us to do?"

"I'll be right there!" Aoi composed herself and headed for the sickroom at a trot.

Chapter 5

**JUNIOR HIGH AND
HIGH SCHOOL ★ TALES
OF KIMETSU ACADEMY!!**

Kimetsu Academy Junior High and High School was an utterly average school beloved by the residents of Kimetsu. It wasn't particularly academic, nor was it a school for delinquents.

The school was decidedly not average in just *one* way. For some reason, the place was full of problem students.

"You want to quit the disciplinary committee?"

"Yeah." Zenitsu nodded glumly after sharing his heartfelt feelings with Tanjiro behind the school building at lunch.

Once again, he had carried out the morning uniform check at this problem academy, and now he was the human equivalent of a wrung-out rag.

Whether it was Inosuke Hashibira, the boy who'd caused a stir in the media for being raised by wild boars rather than wolves (shirt buttons undone, bare feet, no bag other than his lunch); or the volleyball team captain Susamaru (always carrying a metal kemari ball); or the scariest bleached blonde Ume (hates ugliness, uniform modification; also, sexy); or her older brother (extremely

hot for his sister and way, way strong at fighting), they had all absurdly roughed up Zenitsu, and now both his mind and body were a ragged mess.

"I just can't anymore. I never even wanted to do this to begin with. They just went and decided on the committee members on a day I happened to be out from school." Zenitsu sniffled. "I mean, me being on the disciplinary committee at this school, there's just no way. I mean, ever. It just won't work."

"I think you're a good fit for the committee, though," Tanjiro remarked, lowering his eyebrows in concern. "You're always so nice and all. I mean, come on, you even overlooked these earrings that were a keepsake of my father."

Tanjiro was just that kindhearted of a friend, but Zenitsu glared in return.

"Then *you* do it! *You* be on the disciplinary committee instead of me!"

"Hmm. I have to help out at the bakery in the mornings, though."

Tanjiro's family owned a popular bakery and baked about a thousand buns and loaves every morning. Not many knew that Tanjiro himself preferred rice to bread and ate a traditional Japanese breakfast every day.

Incidentally, his younger sister Nezuko Kamado was not only a great beauty, but also always had a baguette in her mouth. Because of that, people would whisper, "If you bump into someone at the corner where Kamado's is, you'll receive a blessing—the shojo manga-esque experience of running into a beautiful girl with bread in her mouth!"

No one had achieved that dream thus far, however. The onus lay with a certain person who burned with such (one-sided) passion for Nezuko that he watched over her from behind an electrical pole, whether she was going to or coming home from school. Normally a pathetic weakling, Zenitsu demonstrated demon-like strength when it came to Nezuko Kamado.

"At least help me quit the disciplinary committee!" Zenitsu begged.

"Can't you just tell Mr. Tomioka you're quitting?" Tanjiro asked naively.

Zenitsu made a face like there was nothing more distasteful to him in this world.

"There's no way he'll actually listen to me! Every time I try to tell him I'm quitting, he yells about how I'm supposed to dye my hair black and punches me! I mean, is he even for real?"

Giyu Tomioka, gym teacher and faculty advisor to the disciplinary committee, was always exceedingly sullen and

grumpy—and because he was faster with his fists than his words, the majority of students were afraid of him, outside of Tanjiro and an exclusive few.

Countless PTA meetings had been held with the "Tomioka problem" taking up the entire agenda, to the point where the group had transformed from the Parent-Teacher Association into something more like the Parent-Tomioka Association.

The man himself was probably clueless and had only the vaguest sense that he was in danger of dismissal. There was a rumor that he'd rescued and adopted a kitten he found on a rainy day, so maybe he was a surprisingly good guy. But the veracity of this was far from certain, and it didn't lead to any real improvement in his reputation.

"But, I mean, you have to go through Mr. Tomioka—"

"I *told* you! I've tried so many times!" Zenitsu shouted in annoyance. "I keep telling him, but he won't listen to me! That guy! Hits me every time I talk to him! Even if I just go near him to talk, he hits me! Come on! What the heck?! This guy! How is he even a teacher! Tomioehhh—"

"Zenitsu?!" Tanjiro cried.

Just saying Tomioka's name made Zenitsu almost vomit. He had developed a Tomioka allergy at long last. He was at a loss to discover that the darkness in his heart was indeed so black.

Perhaps realizing the true seriousness of the issue, Tanjiro said, "Okay. How about this, Zenitsu? We'll go talk to Mr. Tomioka when he's in a good mood. I'll come with you."

"When he's in a good mood?" Zenitsu frowned. "Is he ever?"

Maybe on paydays? Or Casual Friday? Or a day when he had a date? (Wait. Did he even have someone to go out with?) Whatever it was, Zenitsu couldn't begin to imagine Tomioka in a good mood. He didn't even want to, actually. He shook his head and tried to shake these thoughts away.

"Salmon and daikon," Tanjiro announced crisply.

"Huh?" Zenitsu said.

"Mr. Tomioka loves salmon stewed with daikon."

"What? Huh? How do you know that? You... You're kind of scary."

"The truth is, Giyu—I mean, Mr. Tomioka's been a regular at our bakery since before I started at this school." Tanjiro had just happened to overhear a conversation between him and another regular. According to the information he had obtained there...

"I guess he smiles just a bit when he's eating salmon with daikon. But only then."

"Creepy! He smiles?!" Zenitsu let out an exaggerated shudder. "That man can smile?!"

"Listen, Zenitsu," Tanjiro said patiently. "Mr. Tomioka has the fish every day in the cafeteria. And today, the main dish is…"

"No way." Finally serious, Zenitsu stared at Tanjiro.

His classmate nodded firmly. "Salmon stewed with daikon."

"Tanjirooooooooo!" Zenitsu embraced Tanjiro triumphantly, overwhelmed with emotion. Tears streamed down his face. "You really are a true friend!"

"Ow, Zenitsu."

"Now that that's settled, let's get to the cafeteria already!" Zenitsu urged his friend.

They headed to the dining hall in high spirits.

Tomioka was sitting alone at a table near the window. The day's fish dish sat on the tray in front of him. Zenitsu and Tanjiro stood exactly diagonally behind Tomioka, so they couldn't see his face, but the look on it had to have been an expression of never-before-seen bliss.

Tanjiro nodded silently, and Zenitsu returned the nod.

He walked over to Tomioka's side and managed to shout without vomiting, "Mr. Tomioka! I need to talk to you!"

Tomioka looked over his shoulder. "Agatsuma."

"I'm quitting the disci—"

"When are you going to dye your hair black?!"

Before Zenitsu could finish his sentence, a straight right landed on his cheek at unprecedented speed. There wasn't a hint of the joy of salmon stewed with daikon in this punch. In fact, the look on Tomioka's face spoke more of hatred or a deep-seated resentment.

"You're setting a bad example as a member of the disciplinary committee. Go and dye it black right now," his teacher ordered him coldly.

Zenitsu crumpled to the ground soundlessly. *W-why? How? Doesn't stewed salmon and daikon mean smiles?* he asked himself, his mind hazy.

Feeling disconnected, he saw Tanjiro racing over to him and the tray that Tomioka had been eating from. Unfortunately, what was in the dish with the wave pattern on the tray was not salmon stewed with daikon but...

I-it can't be... Yellowtail with daikon? Of course... Resentment toward Tanjiro filled Zenitsu's heart as he lost consciousness.

"I really am so sorry, Zenitsu! I didn't know!" Tanjiro bowed deeply when he came to pick Zenitsu up from the nurse's room after school.

"No. How could you have known?" Zenitsu shook his head lifelessly in the bed. "It's not your fault that the good salmon was suddenly replaced by yellowtail. If anything is to blame, it'd be my bad luck... Ha ha ha ha ha!"

"Zenitsu," Tanjiro murmured.

Zenitsu looked out the window, his gaze distant.

Tanjiro furrowed his brow, pained, and then forced a cheerful smile onto his face. "Hey, Zenitsu? I've been thinking..."

"Huh?" Zenitsu didn't so much as glance at him.

"Why don't you talk to a teacher besides Mr. Tomioka?"

"A teacher besides Mr. T—urp. Him?" Zenitsu hurriedly replaced the name that nearly made him throw up. "Like who?"

"Hmm." Tanjiro thought for a second. "Maybe the art teacher, Mr. Uzui?"

"Nope!" Zenitsu shook his head, firmly. "A big fat nope to the gang teacher! I hate him! I super seriously hate that guy!"

"Okay. Mr. Kyogai. The music teacher."

"Mr. Kyogai gets sick just looking at you, though!"

"Hm?"

Tanjiro cocked his head to one side curiously, not a bit aware of how unimaginably tone-deaf he was, before he frowned in thought again. Then his face lit up.

"I know! Mr. Rengoku!"

"That's it!" Zenitsu cried, jumping down from the nurse's room bed. "Mr. Rengoku's so powerful a character, there's no way he'd lose out to Mr. T—that teacher! And he's a pretty good guy!"

Kyojuro Rengoku was a passionate teacher, a lover of history, and full of love for his students. Although he had a slight tendency not to listen to what people were saying, he was very popular with the students. He was far and away number one on the surveyed list of favorite teachers at Kimetsu Academy.

There may or may not have been some rather stalker-ish opinions in that survey like, "Those muscular arms bursting from the rolled-up sleeves of his button-up shirt slay me" and "I want to be the pin on his necktie" and "I hope he's always so young, hot, and strong." Given his youthful good looks, he was constantly being brought new potential marriage matches, and it must have been a bit of work to turn them all down.

"But where would Mr. Rengoku be at this time of day?" Zenitsu wondered.

"Not in the teachers' room?" Tanjiro replied.

"If you're looking for Mr. Rengoku, he's in the library."

"Wha?!"

At the sudden voice from the bed beside him, Zenitsu almost jumped out of his skin. The curtain between the beds slid back just a bit, and a boy with a grumpy look on his face poked his head out.

"Oh... H-hey there." Zenitsu bowed his head, somewhat freaked out.

"I'm sorry. We were being loud," Tanjiro apologized sincerely.

The grumpy look on the boy's face remained. "If you know that, then get out already. The thing I hate the most is people interfering in this precious time when I lie here alone and sense the aura of Ms. Tamayo working in the nurse's room through the curtain!" he spat, and yanked the curtain closed.

Almost at the same time, the curtain on the other side of the bed was pulled open, and the school doctor, Ms. Tamayo, poked her head in.

"Oh my, Agatsuma," she said softly. "You're awake. Wonderful."

"Y-yes. Thank you."

"You look better, but don't push yourself. Stay in bed for another half an hour, okay?" Tamayo smiled gently, face full of compassion.

DEMON SLAYER: KIMETSU NO YAIBA — THE FLOWER OF HAPPINESS

Meanwhile, he could sense a resentful "hurry up and go" coming loud and clear through the white curtain on the other side, with something approaching murderous thoughts.

"I-I'm all better now, so I'll be on my way!" Zenitsu yelped. "Thank you so much!"

He and Tanjiro hurriedly thanked Ms. Tamayo and left the nurse's room like it was on fire.

That had to have been Yushiro, "master of the nurse's room." Having spent overwhelmingly more hours in the nurse's room than in the classroom, this student wouldn't allow anyone else to get near the place, even if they were seriously ill. No one at Kimetsu Academy knew what grade he was in, what class, or even how old he was.

When they reached the library, the teacher in question was just coming out.

"Mr. Rengok—" Zenitsu started.

"Oh ho! What's wrong? You need me, boys?" the history teacher replied, with a charming and cheerful smile.

In his arms, he held books with titles that seemed like stand-alone jokes: *Go For It! Bento Man!*, *365 Days of Super Tasty Bento*, *Bento to Make Kids Rejoice*.

"You ask him!"

"But this is *your* thing, Zenitsu!"

Zenitsu and Tanjiro silently pushed each other to be the one to speak.

Rengoku didn't notice the strange expressions on their faces. It wasn't so much that he was insensitive, he was just more of a big-picture kind of person and not the type to pick up on subtle cues.

Left with no choice, Tanjiro said, "Um. I thought you lived at home, Mr. Rengoku? Er. Are you actually married?"

"No! I live with my mother, father, and little brother! I'm not married! What of it, young Kamado?"

"Do you make your own bento lunches?" Tanjiro asked.

"Oh, these?" Rengoku finally guessed what Tanjiro was getting at and flashed his snowy-white teeth at them. "My mother has been busy with work lately. I thought I would make my little brother's lunches for her. I know I can't make anything as good as she makes, but I wanted to at least cook something that would make Senjuro happy."

When they pulled back the curtain, the truth turned out

to be nothing of consequence. In fact, this answer only made Rengoku even more likable. This was a departure from Tomioka, whose likability slipped downward every time anyone spoke to him.

"How about it?" the history teacher asked. "Are you boys interested in trying to make bento too? If you want, you can come to my house right now!"

"N-no. We just wanted to talk to you." Tanjiro was flustered at this casual invitation from their teacher. "Right, Zenitsu?"

"Y-yeah. That's right. The truth is, it's about Mr. Tomioka," Zenitsu started.

"Tomioka? You mean my colleague Giyu Tomioka?"

"Yes. I actually want to quit the disciplinary committee, but Mr. Tomioka won't listen to a word I say." Zenitsu told him about the incident in the cafeteria.

"Hmm." Rengoku listened with an unusually serious look on his face.

"Salmon stewed with daikon would be good too!" he opined cheerfully. "The combination of fish and vegetables is a healthy one, and not only that, daikon is in season. Seasonal food is healthy food! High nutritional value!"

"Huh?"

"Uh…um."

"Boys, we'll stop by the supermarket and then head to my house. Wait. Better to get daikon at the greengrocer. Salmon at the fishmonger!"

"But that's not what we—"

"I'll lend you both aprons. Don't worry about that!"

"No!" Zenitsu cried.

"Mr. Rengoku, salmon stewed with daikon isn't really that great for bento, though," Tanjiro noted. "If you don't make sure it's walled off in its own section, the rice'll end up all soggy."

"Wait. Not you too!" Zenitsu yelped, betrayal on his face.

"I see." Rengoku nodded thoughtfully. "We'll have to make rice too! Main dishes alone are unbalanced!"

"What about cooking the rice with some vegetables?" Tanjiro suggested.

"Great idea!" the history teacher cried. "Okay! We'll stop by the rice shop!"

"No, but that's not—" Zenitsu protested.

"Don't be shy! Establishing lines of communication with students is an important part of a teacher's job!"

"But I just want to quit the disciplinary committee!" Zenitsu wailed.

A history teacher—who ignored what other people were saying even more than a certain other teacher—had toyed with him. A friend had been surprisingly idiotic. Zenitsu's evening wore on.

"I... I thought Mr. Rengoku would at least listen to me."

At the restaurant Aoi, not too far from Kimetsu Academy, Zenitsu asked for an iced coffee and a dessert to cleanse his palate. He slumped over to rest his head on the table.

Mr. Rengoku seemed like the type of person who could master anything, but it turned out that he was a horrible cook. Not only that, but because he'd produced failure after failure with such innocence and good cheer, Zenitsu hadn't been able to get angry at him. But he had been angry, and his taste buds had gotten all twisted up from too much taste testing. Each attempt at salmon stewed with daikon tasted so foul that Zenitsu was certain every bite would be his last. He had no interest in crossing paths with daikon or salmon for a while.

"Plus, just when I thought we were finally free, we get wrung out in Mr. Rengoku's dad's kendo class," he moaned.

"Come on, now. Mr. Rengoku's dad and Senjuro were really happy to have us join in, so it all worked out, right?" Tanjiro, the perfect honors student, replied.

Zenitsu glared at Tanjiro bitterly. "What about my problem?! I'm still stuck on the disciplinary committee!"

"Oh, that. Right." Tanjiro smiled sheepishly. "I'm sorry. I forgot."

Of course he forgot.

"It's hell for me again tomorrow morning. Aah, I wish I could just run away. I want to go to a world that doesn't have Tomi—that man in it."

Zenitsu kept grumbling and whining even after his order came. As Tanjiro tried in vain to console him, the restaurant's star attraction, Aoi Kanzaki, returned with another academy student, Shinobu Kocho, in tow.

"Oh my! Tanjiro and Zenitsu, both here!" she said. "It's good to see you. I'll make some fresh tea right now. Please have a seat, Shinobu. Is *anmitsu* with cream and *shiratama* dumplings all right?"

"Yes." Shinobu nodded. "Heavy on the brown sugar syrup."

High school second-year Aoi was in the flower-arranging club. High school third-year Shinobu belonged to both the pharmacology club and the fencing team.

Both girls were beautiful, but Shinobu in particular was so gorgeous that she was constantly fielding offers from talent and modeling agencies. On top of that, her grades were always the best in her class. With her wins at fencing tournaments and other accomplishments, Shinobu was more than just a cute girl—she took the title of Miss Kimetsu every year.

On the other hand, there were also strange rumors. Things like how she made dangerous drugs with no taste or smell in pharmacology club, or how she had more than a few teachers essentially under her thumb, or how *the* Tomioka was one of those teachers.

The nickname a very few whispered was "Princess of Poison." Naturally, Zenitsu didn't take any of that talk seriously for one simple reason.

There's no way someone this pretty could be a bad person.

"What's the matter? You look blue. I'm here to listen if you want to talk," Shinobu said with concern as she sat down at their table.

Zenitsu ogled her indiscreetly. There was no way someone this kind and gentle could be a scary person. Those rumors were just nonsense spread by people who were jealous of her looks and talents.

"The truth is…" He told her about his current struggle.

Shinobu listened attentively, nodding every so often. Then she said, "I think that Mr. Tomioka has really high hopes for you, Zenitsu."

"High hopes?" He frowned.

Shinobu smiled gently. "Because Mr. Tomioka is the way he is, a lot of students misunderstand him. They even hate him, so the disciplinary committee is always shorthanded; people are constantly leaving it. You've really stuck by Mr. Tomioka, haven't you, Zenitsu? I think, deep down, that makes him so happy."

"No, but it's not like I stayed because I want to." He'd just been forced to do what the teacher told him to, bound by a collar called violence.

"Mr. Tomioka actually once said to me, 'Agamatsu's doing a good job,'" she told him.

"Um. Mr. Tomioka said that?" Zenitsu stared at Shinobu in disbelief.

Perhaps because of her beauty—or perhaps because the Tomioka she spoke of was somehow magnificent, like she was

talking about an alter ego—Zenitsu was able to say the name without vomiting.

"I think that the work of the disciplinary committee is really difficult. But you and the others are out there doing it, keeping the peace at our school." The goddess of the academy narrowed her eyes with a beautiful smile.

She gently placed her hand on Zenitsu's. He wasn't sure if it was her shampoo or some fragrance she wore, but she smelled indescribably good.

"Keep fighting the good fight, Zenitsu." She squeezed his hand. "I'm cheering for you most of all."

"Okaaaaaaay!!"

Zenitsu was so excited, blood nearly spurted from his nose.

"You just leave it to old Zenitsu here!" he assured her. In his mind, he shouted, *Joy!! Aaaah, such bliss!* and leaped up to the heavens.

Aoi came along with more tea and a bowl of anmitsu, and she eyed Shinobu and Zenitsu with a knowing look on her face.

"I don't know if I should mention this," she said in a quiet voice. "But you are the thirtieth person this month, Zenitsu, that Shinobu is cheering for most of all. I think it would be better for you if you were not to take it too seriously."

Naturally, however, Zenitsu heard not a word of this.

"That's great, huh, Zenitsu? You really are a good fit for the disciplinary committee. Good luck!" Tanjiro said with a grin, but Zenitsu didn't hear this either.

Aoi let out an exasperated sigh.

Okay! I'll do it! I'll do it for her! Because I'm the boy Shinobu's cheering for most of all!! Zenitsu, with his simple soul, vowed passionately in his heart.

"Mr. Tomioka!"

The next morning, when Zenitsu spotted Tomioka doing uniform checks in front of the school gates, he raced over to him with a smile on his face. Tomioka was wearing a tracksuit that day. His gym whistle hung around his neck, and his beloved bamboo sword was in hand.

"Mr. Tomioka! I made an appointment at the salon for Saturday!" Zenitsu announced in a loud voice, eyes shining like he had been reborn. "I'll dye my hair black and work even

harder as a member of the disciplinary committee! I hope I can count on your guidance and support—"

"Quiet, you!"

"Bu—?!"

Zenitsu took an impossible hit from Tomioka and went sailing through the air.

"No shouting at school," the teacher told him.

This... It doesn't make any sense.

Zenitsu crumpled to the ground, not even able to shed tears.

Later, at lunch...

"Tanjrooo! I want to quit the disciplinary committee already!" Zenitsu cried in anguish. "I hate it!! I mean, Tomi—hrk!"

"Zenitsu..." Tanjiro sighed.

Incidentally, a few days later...

"I stopped you from hemorrhaging committee members you so desperately need, so please give my team more gym space to use next month, okay, Mr. Tomioka?"

Shinobu reportedly threatened the teacher—or perhaps made a request of him with an extremely innocent look on her face. Hearing this, Zenitsu took to his bed for three whole days, but that is a different story.

All in all, it was another peaceful day at Kimetsu Academy Junior High and High School (except for one person).

Afterword
KOYOHARU GOTOUGE

Thanks for reading.

    I was trying on glasses the other day, and the clerk told me that it's fashionable to wear them a little low on your face. So I pushed them all the way to the end of my nose, and in return, I got a pained smile and the comment that there are limits as to how low. That's me, Gotouge.

    Did you enjoy the book?

    This is the first time I've gotten to draw illustrations for a book, and I was both excited and nervous about it.

    I hope you've upped your immune-system strength with all this reading fun, so you can enjoy your days free of colds—healthy and happy.

Afterword
AYA YAJIMA

I love *Demon Slayer: Kimetsu no Yaiba*. I really love it. I love it so much I worry a little about myself. I honestly adore it.

So when I was approached about novelizing the series, I was over the moon, shrieking to myself. (Naturally, a high-pitched, annoying nasal whine.)

Koyoharu Gotouge, thank you so, so very much for taking the time when you were so busy with the series and anime adaptation to make your diligent checks of the manuscript, your incredibly powerful illustrations, and the cover that I can only describe as wonderful.

When you told me Master Jigoro's name, I was so delighted that I fell prostrate before my computer.

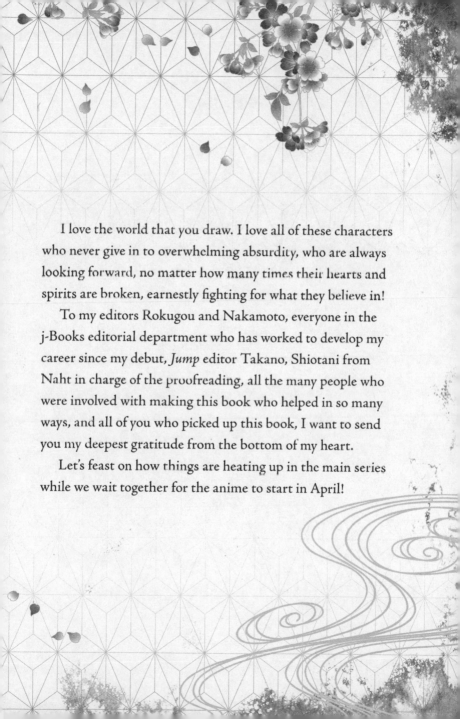

I love the world that you draw. I love all of these characters who never give in to overwhelming absurdity, who are always looking forward, no matter how many times their hearts and spirits are broken, earnestly fighting for what they believe in!

To my editors Rokugou and Nakamoto, everyone in the j-Books editorial department who has worked to develop my career since my debut, *Jump* editor Takano, Shiotani from Naht in charge of the proofreading, all the many people who were involved with making this book who helped in so many ways, and all of you who picked up this book, I want to send you my deepest gratitude from the bottom of my heart.

Let's feast on how things are heating up in the main series while we wait together for the anime to start in April!